Rules of Darkness

Rules of Darkness

by

Tia Fanning

Resplendence Publishing, LLC
http://www.resplendencepublishing.com

Resplendence Publishing, LLC
P.O. Box 992
Edgewater, Florida, 32132

Rules of Darkness
Copyright © 2007, Tia Fanning
Edited by Jessica Berry and Tiffany Mason
Cover art by Rika Singh
Print format ISBN: 978-0-9795721-8-0
Electronic format ISBN: 978-0-9797946-7-4

Warning: All rights reserved. The unauthorized reproduction or distribution of this copyrighted work is illegal. Criminal copyright infringement, including infringement without monetary gain, is investigated by the FBI and is punishable by up to 5 years in federal prison and a fine of $250,000.

Electronic release: October, 2007
Trade paperback printing: November, 2007, February 2008, August 2008.

This is a work of fiction. Names, characters, places, and occurrences are a product of the author's imagination. Any resemblance to actual persons, living or dead, places, or occurrences, is purely coincidental.

To my publishers, Leigh and Jess.

Chapter One

There are rules for people like me.

That's what my great-grandmother used to say. She'd say, "Katia, you are special, so it is most important you follow the rules. The rules will keep you safe."

Even before there were rules, there were signs.

It started with my conception. I was a blessing wrought from a brutal crime forced upon my young mother as she walked home alone one eve. The man who planted his seed was *touched in the mind* as they used to say, and had escaped from the nearby asylum. He came upon my mother, did his deed and left, muttering that he could not kill the woman with the river of midnight hair.

My great-grandma used to tell me that all I was, and all I would become, began then.

That was the first sign.

Then, on a cold night during the month of the Epiphany, my mother went into premature labor. Beneath a clear star-filled sky and a Lilith moon, she laid on a pile of blankets next to a fire, her body wracked in pain. The elders had gathered to see what kind of child she'd bring forth.

The whole village knew of the circumstances that brought my mother to that point, and they knew she would not live to see the morning, for my great-grandmother, a powerful seer, had read it in the cards. Even in those so-called *modern times*, my people still followed the old ways. Not that it mattered, for our kind would've never considered stepping foot in any hospital.

So as my mother gave me life, she lost hers, only living long enough to name me "Katia".

That was the second sign.

My great-grandmother saw to my care and found another woman suckling to give me milk. She had done this before, as my mother's mother had met the same fate. As my eyes turned from blue to blue hazel, she often said she knew then, if the other two signs had not been enough, that I was special.

"Four colors. Your eyes hold all of nature. The green of the sacred tree, the gold of sand and stone, the blue of sky and water, but most importantly, you have the ring of shadow that binds them all. They will flock to you, thinking you are their way to heaven. If they live, lay your hands upon them and grant them peace. But never with the dead."

That was the third sign… and my first rule.

I never knew who "they" were until I was five. It was a beautiful autumn day and I wandered through the woods alone, enjoying the sunbeams dancing through the canopy of trees as I picked berries. A woman appeared then, naked and lost, not only in the forest, but also in the maze of voices that floated around in her head. I could hear them whispering.

We made eye contact.

She stumbled toward me, grabbing onto flimsy bushes that refused to hold her weight, until finally she collapsed at my feet. Rising to her knees, she wrapped her arms around me and pulled me close, holding me as one would their own child.

At first, I stood dumbfounded, unable to speak. I wondered if she was a patient of the nearby hospital—the place where mean doctors locked people away in chains and opened their skulls with butcher knives.

Then my great-grandma's words came to me.

They will flock to you, thinking you are their way to heaven. If they live, lay your hands upon them…

I hugged her back. "Go in peace."

Sobbing, the woman withdrew. I watched her eyes as her mind collected the many people in her head and merged them into one being.

She looked down at her bare body, then back at me. "Where am I?"

I shrugged.

"Little girl, may I borrow your cape?"

I untied it from my shoulders and handed it to her.

"Thank you, for everything," she whispered and walked away.

Great-grandma was upset when I came home without my cloak. When I explained what happened, she just patted my head, telling me that it was time for me to learn all the rules.

For many sheltered years, I heard them, memorized them, studied them and practiced them. Then one day, when I was sixteen, my great-grandmother died and I was alone in the world. That very night, under the cover of darkness, I fled my village forever, and even broke a rule while doing so.

It was a full moon.

I ran away from my life, away from all I'd ever known, away from my arranged betrothal. I ran from my destiny, for it was too much for me to bear.

I ended up traveling the world, wanting nothing more than to be *alone*. I survived by taking odd jobs and living off the generosity of others until I saved up enough money to move on, or attracted enough lost to make staying dangerous to the people around me.

Finally, I settled down here in America and went to school. I became an artist and have done well for myself. Very well. I have no regrets except for the love I left behind.

But no matter how far I ran from home, the rules of my life stayed close. Twelve rules, just like the twelve months in a year:

- *Never walk the forest at night when the moon is full.*
- *Never look into a dark mirror.*
- *Never glance into a graveyard as you pass it.*
- *If you should see an unknown light reflect in the eyes of an animal, leave immediately.*
- *Should you hear three unseen knocks, leave immediately.*
- *Never pick up random objects that lay outside on the ground.*
- *Never keep any object if you don't know its origin.*
- *Avoid objects and places that have a violent history or were created before time written.*
- *Never seek out the lost. Let them come to you.*
- *Never allow someone to tell you your future.*
- *Never tell anyone of your gifts.*
- *And most importantly—never touch the dead. Not in any form.*

You might wonder why I'm giving you my life story, and my answer to you would be because it is necessary. It is the only way you can understand how I found myself where I am now... standing before my French doors, looking through the glass at a pale, dark-haired teen with empty black eyes and the gaping mouth of death.

He wants me to let him in.

Chapter Two

Three weeks ago, I bought a house. It's just a simple cabin-like structure situated off a lake in a remote forest area. I like it here. It's a great place to think, to create art, and there are no people around. Hell, the nearest city is miles and miles away.

However, being new to the area, I'm still ignorant of all the locations that would violate my life's rules. Last Tuesday, as I returned from the grocery store in town, I'd glanced out my passenger window to something I thought was a park. I quickly discovered it was a graveyard.

I had made similar mistakes in the past, but this time, the site contained a new person, one who had neither found rest nor left the place that held his corpse. And it was too late for me to pretend I didn't see him. He knew I did.

My great-grandma used to say the spirits who couldn't find peace in death usually strayed from their bodies, roaming the earth until they found closure. But if the timing was right, or wrong in my case, it was possible to find a spirit still in attendance near their body.

Ghosts are not stupid. They know they're dead. And they understand that the majority of the population will not be able to acknowledge them on a tangible level. But when they find someone who can see them, they attach themselves to that person, wanting that person to help them find rest.

That's what happened to me exactly one week ago.

You see, ghosts move in a time that is different from ours. Depending on their power, which is fueled by their emotional state and other unknown rules that govern their existence, it's possible for their time to speed ahead of ours, or slow up to what could equate to years in our reality.

For this kid, it had taken him a week to move from the graveyard to my back deck.

I wish it had been years.

He is distraught, so his power is greater.

When a person such as myself is haunted, we suffer the full effects of it. We see it, we feel it—our brains don't rationalize it out as a natural, explainable occurrence. So, as my great-grandma used to say, life only gets worse when an unsettled spirit is in it.

And for entities that have all eternity to figure out what kept them on this plane of existence, they're remarkably impatient.

They want to move on, and they want to do it now. And they want *you* to make it happen. Fail them in that, and see what they can do. You may not believe it, or may not *want* to believe it, but they can easily kill you.

Charlie, my very large guard dog, lumbered to my side, his long claws clicking on the hard wood floor. With fur standing on end across his arched back, he bared his teeth and snarled at the specter on the other side of the paneled glass.

Unfortunately, the dead kid is more powerful than both of us put together.

I brushed my hand across my dog's head. "Down boy," I murmured.

Charlie gave a deep bark, protesting my command.

"I know. I see him too. You're a good boy for trying to protect me."

Rules of Darkness

Ghosts are around us all the time, day and night. On the street, on the subway—sometimes even living with us. The average person cannot see them, but almost every animal can.

Humans in general live a life of ignorant bliss, fairly unaware of the dark things that go on around them—and there are many dark things in this world. I, on the other hand, have to live a life of avoidance. Anytime I see a spirit, I duck my head and pretend I don't. This usually works for me. And as long as I avoid ancient sites, museums, and other old buildings, I can lead a somewhat normal life.

Which reminded me...

Gathering as much courage as I could, and what I lacked, I substituted with false bravado, I took a step forward and looked into the kid's ink-like eyes.

"I can't help you. I don't have anything in the house you can use to communicate."

I wasn't lying. There was nothing in my house for him to use. I wouldn't allow things into my haven that produced white noise or have a speaker. No TV, no radio, no phone. And God knows I'd never have the medium objects around such as tarot cards or an Ouija board. Never would I send an open invitation to the unsettled, or possibly even more dangerous, the fallen ones.

The kid slowly moved his gaping mouth wider, but as I expected, no sound came out. He kept trying, showing me his thick black tongue. His expression reminded me of a fish taken out of water and set on the deck to die.

Frustration fed him power. The hanging wind chimes pinged violently as the air picked up speed around the spirit. A patio chair blew over.

I shook my head slowly. "I'm sorry. Please leave and find someone else to help you," I whispered.

The wind subsided some.

For the first time, I really looked at the kid. He suddenly seemed like a lost little boy with his shaggy hair and big sad eyes... well, a scary, freaky, dead little boy. But despite my overwhelming fear, I felt bad about the whole thing.

I wondered how he died and why he didn't move on.

No, I shouldn't wonder such things. I mustn't get attached.

The kid was dangerous to me. He could kill me. Worse, he might touch me, and I could lose my soul.

Avoid him—ignore him, that's what I needed to do. Maybe he'd just leave. However, the way my luck was going, he'd probably stay put and try to find a way into the house.

I glanced at the door. Crap! Was the door even locked?

The kid must have read my mind. Agonizingly slow, he lifted his stiff arm, his talon like fingers curling as he reached for the handle.

Charlie barked and jumped forward.

I too made a dash for the door.

Out of the way, Charlie!

Tripping over my dog's large body, I fell on my hands and knees, hitting the hard wood floor with a thud.

Shit!

Charlie was attacking the door, jumping, growling, barking and hitting his paws against the glass. Scrambling forth, I flung my hand out to grab a hold of the dead bolt's latch. Before I could get a solid grip, Charlie collided with my arm and my fingers fumbled, sliding off the small metal piece.

"Move! Move!"

With all my strength, I pushed the dog out of the way. I heard him yelp as I reached up and locked the door.

Silence.

Thank you, Lord.

Sitting on the floor, I didn't move. I didn't dare breathe. Charlie was also frozen in place, but he continued

Rules of Darkness

to stare past me, his eyes reflecting a light unnatural. He whimpered.

I followed Charlie's gaze through the glass.

Big mistake.

The kid's lips shriveled up. His face melted into a mask of horrific rage as his hair flew back and razor sharp teeth spouted out, two inches long.

The patio table catapulted off the deck, followed instantly by the chairs. The French doors rattled as three booming knocks echoed through the house. Several windowpanes shattered. Glass rained upon me.

The kid had never moved. Wrath fueled his power and manifested his thoughts.

Shit!

Charlie barked furiously as I clambered back, sliding across the floor.

The rule! Three unseen knocks! I had to get out of there.

Three more knocks radiated, accompanied by the sound of splintering wood. What little glass was left imploded, then exploded, and flew through the air. A gust of howling wind rushed in. The doors shook on their hinges.

I got to my feet and ran for the living room, Charlie following at my heels.

Three thundering knocks behind me.

Three pounding knocks before me.

Swinging the front door open, I collided into a rock hard wall of male. I stumbled back and fell on my ass. Charlie danced around me in excitement.

I looked up.

The sight that met my eyes almost made me lose the contents of my stomach. There stood the one man in the world who might actually be more dangerous to me than the damn kid on my back porch. Twelve years might have passed, but I knew him all the same. I could never forget him.

"Stoyan." I whispered.

Stoyan silently stared at me with cold eyes.

It couldn't be.

Despite the hurricane force winds, the glass, wood, and other debris flying around my house, not to mention the ghost trying to break through my French doors to kill me, I could not find the strength to lift myself off the floor. And the more I looked at the jilted fiancé on my front step, the more I realized that it would be easier to die now than have to face my past.

Hell, what did I have to live for anyway?

Come on kid...

Three exploding knocks. Chunks of wood fell, the clatter of it resounding in the wind. I knew the door would not sustain another hit. The ghost would soon be in the house.

Tears brimmed behind my lashes and I looked down. If death was on its way to claim me as I hoped, wished, prayed, and greatly suspected from the sounds behind me, this moment was to be my last.

And the last thing I'd see was Stoyan.

I couldn't believe it.

My world instantly shattered into a million pieces. I never thought I'd see him again. For the sake of my sanity, my heart, and my very way of life, I never *wanted* to see him again.

Black boots and the hem of his jeans came into view, stopping before me. I mumbled a prayer to the good Lord asking that the ghost not touch me when he killed me, and that my death be quick and painless. As I begged for entrance into Heaven, I also asked God to spare Stoyan. I wasn't even ready to face my ex in paradise.

"*Siligul galak adda gidum, ebitum wasuzah,*" Stoyan chanted. I lifted my head in time to see him raise his arm. "*Ribarra!*"

A sudden burst of energy, then everything stilled and fell silent.

Rules of Darkness

Damn! Damn! Damn!

He had banished the ghost.

I couldn't decipher Stoyan's words, but their sound was familiar, as I had heard the ancient speech before as a child. But only Stoyan, and others with his gifts, knew their true meaning.

He lowered his arm and turned his intense gaze on me.

I read so much there. Pain, disappointment, anger, accusation. He thought I betrayed him. In a way, I guess I did. After all, when I left my village behind twelve years ago, I left the promise of our love behind too. But sometimes in life, we all have to make hard decisions and do what we think is best.

Though it broke my heart to know that I'd never see him again, running away had been what was best for me. I had to save myself. And to save myself, I had to lose myself. And by losing myself, I found myself.

I hoped he could understand that.

My dog growled. Stoyan shifted his eyes to Charlie, who in turn, whimpered and proceeded out the front door.

Damn traitor.

My ex-betrothed seemed to get angrier as the silent seconds passed. If his expression showed anything, either he didn't get the letter I left him when I ran away, or he didn't accept my reasons for leaving.

"I received your letter," he murmured in our people's tongue.

Could everybody read my mind?

The sound of my native language reminded me that I once lived in another world, in another time, as another Katia.

Memories of Stoyan assaulted me and I bowed my head again, no longer able to face him. There was too much between us. Too much past and too much pain. It hadn't been my intention to hurt him.

"I see shame besets you. You should be ashamed," he remarked.

Indignation swept over my emotional turmoil. "Don't talk to me in that way. I'm not a child anymore," I replied in English. "And who are you to judge me? You have no right."

I would not— *would not*— speak in my people's tongue. After all, I wasn't that person anymore.

He gave an empty laugh. "Oh, Katia, but I do have the right," he flung back in perfect English. "I am your husband."

I shook my head. "No, we were only engaged."

"And one of the elders stood in your place for the matrimonial ceremony. I assure you, we are legally married."

I looked at his hand. He wore a ring.

"That's bullshit," I spat.

Crap like this reminded me why I had no regrets leaving my old life behind. That way of life was simply archaic.

"It is the way of our people, so you know I speak the truth. You can run, you can try to fool yourself, but it still does not change who you are, nor make you any less my *wife*."

Was I supposed to just accept this on his word alone? Was I to cry tears of shame because I *dishonored* my *husband*? Did he expect me to beg for his forgiveness? Well, it'd be a cold day in hell before any of that happened.

"I am less your wife then you believe. Our union has never been consummated. *By the rules of our people*, the ceremony has not been completed."

"We will take care of that small detail soon enough."

I gasped and jumped to my feet. "No. You will not touch me."

Why had he come here? Why couldn't he just let it go?

I saw his body tense. "You ran away from me for no reason. Now that I found you, you would deny me what is mine?"

Mine? No reason?

"You were the one who left first. You left when I was ten. You were the one who wasn't there when I needed you. What kind of a protector are you? Did you think a few letters by mail and a yearly two-week visit would hold me until you returned for our marriage ceremony?"

"Enough!" he commanded.

"No, it's not enough!"

I was so overwhelmed by emotion, my whole body shook. The tears my lashes had managed to keep in check spilled forth.

I turned away from him. "I was the one who lost my best friend when you went away. My only friend. I was the one who was lonely for six years. And when great-grandma died, I was the one alone in the world. You were not there! I was obviously meant to be alone, so alone is how I went into my new life."

"You knew I would come to you if you needed me. You should have sent a letter and waited. Or you should have had someone in the village make a trip to town and phone me. There is no excuse for your actions."

I swung back around and pointed at the door. "Get out!"

Stoyan didn't move.

Hell, I should've just let the friggin ghost in. Death would have been much easier to deal with.

Taking a calming breath, I brushed the tears off my cheeks. "Leave. I don't want you. I don't need you. You are not my husband. I don't care if our marriage was arranged before my birth. Just leave."

Stoyan shook his head. "You are a healer of the lost, and I am your protector," he stated softly. "We are destined. I love you. I know you love me. This is not something you can run from."

If my world shattered the moment he appeared, then his declarations were pounding those fragments to dust. It was too much. If he stayed any longer, there'd be nothing left of me.

Screw it. If he wouldn't leave, then I would.

"Fuck destiny, fuck your love, and fuck you." I spun around to walk away.

"Katia—"

Black dots formed in my dizzy eyes and I fell to my knees.

Stoyan was at my side instantly, gathering me in his strong arms. He still smelled the way I remembered. Woodsy, spicy, intoxicating. His embrace was familiar and comforting, as if twelve long years hadn't passed since I'd last seen him.

Like he'd always been in my life.

But he hadn't. He hadn't been there. He had only just arrived.

I began to sob and tried to push him away. "No, Stoyan. When I needed you, you weren't there. So I left. I am lost to you now."

"Sleep, my love. I will take care of you."

He ran his fingers across my forehead and started murmuring in that ancient language again.

No, no, no…

Chapter Three

I dreamt of wandering through a darkened forest for what seemed like endless hours. Finally, I spotted firelight flickering through the trees and bushes. A scream of pain pierced the air as I stumbled out into a small dirt village filled with assorted stone huts and wooden shacks.

I know this place...Oh, God. I'm home.

Moaning drew my attention. Near the fire lay a young woman in the throes of labor, her face contorted with pain. At the base of the woman's parted legs sat middle-aged woman surrounded by pots of steaming water and blankets. In her hand, she held a sponge.

The village midwife. Roxelana was her name.

Then I noticed my great-grandma. She was on her knees, holding the young woman's hand. With her free hand, great-grandma dipped a rag into a bowl, then dabbed it on the young woman's brow.

No. Please, not this.

I didn't want to watch my mother depart from the world.

Though my mind protested, even demanded that I turn around and leave, or better yet, wake up from this horrible nightmare, my feet moved forward of their own accord, drawing me closer to the scene.

My mother screamed again.

The elders came out from their homes, each making his or her way toward the fire. They gathered a few feet behind my great-grandma. Some I recognized immediately, as familiar fixtures from my youth.

The oldest of the group, a woman with straw white hair that matched milky white eyes, scuttled forth. "Marija, will this be the birth of the girl in your vision?" she croaked.

My great-grandmother laid her hand upon my mother's stomach. "Yes, it is she."

"Grandmother, I cannot do this," my mother cried.

"You can, my child. You are doing well," my great-grandmother soothed.

My mother tossed her head side to side. "Your daughter... my mother... she is here to take me to heaven. Grandmother, she is so pretty. She is calling for me to come with her."

Great-grandmother looked at the group of elders.

Hammu, with his tuft of grey hair and leather skin, nodded. "Your granddaughter speaks the truth. Your daughter is among us."

Great-grandma turned back and brought my mother's hand to her lips. "Not— not yet, my child, my Anya," she stuttered as tears rolled down her cheeks. "Give me this baby first, so when you leave, I will not grow old alone."

Nodding vigorously, my mother bundled her fist tighter around the blanket that covered her body and pushed again, her eyes squeezing shut in the effort.

"The baby comes now," Roxelana said.

Another old woman came forth from the group of elders. Safira put her hand on my great-grandmother's shoulder. "Marija, you knew this day would come. You read it in the cards. Be strong for Anya and let her go."

My mother gave a wrenching scream before her exhausted body went limp, leaving only her chest heaving as she gasped for air. The midwife moved with swift hands. Moments later, baby wails seeped into the night.

Rules of Darkness 23

Roxelana stood and carried the small crying bundle, kneeling beside my great-grandma. Just as she was about to hand the baby over to my mother, the milky-eyed woman stayed the midwife's arm.

"No, the child is special, she mustn't..." the elder trailed off.

Sadly nodding her understanding, Roxelana pulled the baby close and turned to my mother. "You have a beautiful daughter, Anya. She is small, but she is strong. She will live."

My mother didn't reach out for me. "Beautiful," she whispered as her eyelids shuttered closed.

"Anya?" my great-grandmother's voice cracked.

My mother opened her eyes slightly. "May I go now, grandmother?"

My great-grandmother bit her lip and whimpered.

Safira gave her shoulder a squeeze. "Marija..."

Firm resolve formed on great-grandma's face. Grasping my mother's hand tighter, she leaned over and placed a soft kiss on her head. She drew a shaky breath as she lifted up. "Yes, Anya, if you must, you can go. I will miss you." She smoothed my mother's hair as she swallowed her grief. "I love you so much. I am proud of you."

"Do not be sad," my mother murmured, giving a faint smile. "I will see you again soon. I love you. And my baby, Katia..." her voice faded away and her eyes fell closed. Her chest stilled.

There was a moment of heavy silence.

My great-grandmother began shaking. "Anya, oh, my little Anya," she wept, collapsing over my mother's body.

Hammu came upon the woman. "Anya's spirit has departed. Have peace, for it was a beautiful reunion between mother and daughter."

I, my adult self, took no comfort in his words. I crumpled onto the ground, crying so hard I could not find air. Why did I have to see this? Why must I be reminded that I was the bringer of my mother's death?

Strong arms wrapped around my body and started rocking me.

"Shh, Katia. It is not your fault, my love," Stoyan murmured.

"How are you here," I stammered into his shirt, burying myself in his warm scent.

"I came to you."

His concern made me cry even more. "I can't take this. Why must I endure this dream? Why won't I wake up?"

"It is not a dream. It is a vision from the past," he whispered in my ear. "Listen…"

"Marija, take her," I heard Roxelana urge in a broken voice. "See what Anya has given you."

I lifted my head up in time to see my great-grandmother cradle the baby to her chest. The elders gathered close.

"She is a healer," one elder claimed as she laid her hand upon the small bundle.

"And a powerful one," said another, caressing the baby's cheek. "The signs are all here. If her eyes turn—"

"They will," my great-grandma spoke up. "She will be a healer of the mind. She will save the lost ones."

A collective murmuring went through the group. The two elders moved back so the others could place their hands on the baby.

"Not only will the lost come to her, but she will be able to see the unsettled, perhaps even the fallen," Hammu stated.

"Yes, she is powerful, but her gifts came at a great price," said the milky-eyed woman.

Another man with a peppered mane and long beard stepped forth and placed his hand on the infant. "Hmmm, her soul is free. The departed can snatch it from her body.

Rules of Darkness 25

She must never touch the dead in any form. And she must also beware the fallen, for they too will want to claim her."

Gasps of horror filled the air.

"There is more," continued the milky-eyed woman, prying open the baby's hand and frowning.

"No, no, please. Do not say she has moon madness," my great-grandma whispered, shaking her head.

"No, but she carries the scent of the shifters. She must stay away from those inflicted. They will see her as a mate."

"So much for a child," Safira mumbled, caressing the baby's hair. "She will need a protector."

"But who? Those of us left are much too old," the bearded man asked.

My great-grandmother smiled softly. "Fate has already chosen. I have seen him too. He is young, but powerful enough. It will be Stylianos' son, Stoyan."

"But they are no longer of us!" one of the men from the group exclaimed. "You must choose someone else."

The milky-eyed woman waved her hand, "No, Marija is right. Her destiny has been set, her protector chosen. Stylianos may have left us as all the young ones have, but his heart is still here. He will accept his responsibility and has taught his son the same."

"It is true," agreed Hammu. "Does not Stoyan come to us in the summer to learn our ways? Does not Stylianos keep to our traditions? Fate knows what is right."

"He will keep you safe, Katia, if you but let him," my great-grandma told the baby. "You two will share a great love of each other, but you will be stubborn, like my Anya. I can see this. You will push him away, but destiny is not always so easily abandoned."

* * * *

I opened my wet, swollen eyes to darkness, a sob still on my lips. Despite the horrible events I'd just witnessed in my vision dream, I felt an odd sense comfort, something I hadn't felt in a very long time—warm and safe, loved and protected.

Then I realized why.

Stoyan's arm was draped over my side, his fingers splayed across my stomach. His head was next to mine on my pillow, his hot breath caressing my neck.

What made him think it was okay to join me in *my* bed and invade *my* dream?

He drew me closer to him.

I stiffened in his arms, not because it was natural reaction, but because I felt like I should. Like this action would communicate how offended I was at his intrusion into my life.

Stoyan gave a soft chuckle in my ear. "Oh Katia, you are stubborn. Will you fight us forever?"

"If I must," I replied quietly.

"I've waited most of my life to hold you like this."

I scrunched my nose. "What do you mean? When I was child, you held me often."

"True, but I did so the way a brother would hold his sister. Now, I hold you the way a man does his wife."

I let out a skeptical snort. "Do you know how sick that sounds? If you thought me like a sister, then this moment should feel incestuous to you."

Stoyan stroked the hair at my temples. "No, this moment feels right. You were but a child when we met. How else should I have acted?"

I really didn't know how to respond. I mean, ours had been a strange relationship from the get-go. He had been my betrothed since I was six months old, he only eight years old.

For my time growing up with Stoyan, he never did anything unwarranted, never touched in ways he shouldn't, never acted out of order. If anything, he always stood by me, supported me, and even took a beating for me once. He treated me, I suppose, as a brother would his baby sister.

Rules of Darkness   *27*

But when his feelings evolved into something more than platonic, I couldn't say.

"Do you remember when you where fourteen and we had that snow fight?" he asked.

I felt my cheeks grow warm. How could I forget that day? It was one of the most humiliating experiences of my life.

"I don't want to remember."

Stoyan blew out a heavy breath. "I thought you would have gotten over it by now. Did you not forgive me?"

"Yes, but it doesn't mean I want to remember."

However, the memory played in my head anyway. Stoyan had come to visit me during his Christmas break. I was so fascinated by him, so in love, so hopeful for us. We went walking in the forest. Somehow, we ended up in a snowball fight. He tackled me and we tumbled down a snow embankment. I landed on top of him. With labored breath, I stared into his eyes. He was quite a handsome man, but what possessed me to kiss him, I don't know.

"You were so horrified, you practically threw me off you," I muttered.

"It was never like that, Katia. I was a twenty-one year-old man, and you were a fourteen year-old girl."

"Yeah, I remember you saying that then, too," I replied bitterly.

"You were so beautiful and so mature for your age. I almost forgot how young you were. After I pushed you off me, you stood up and dusted the snow from yourself. You stared me down and stated that if we were to be married one day, and if I loved you and you loved me, we should be able to kiss now."

"I know."

"Do you remember my reply?" he murmured in my ear.

Thinking back on it now, I realized it was the most beautiful thing someone could ever say.

Rolling over onto my back, I looked at Stoyan's face. Though shadowed, the moonlight that filtered in through the blinds glittered in his eyes.

I gazed into the sparkles. "You said that real love is worth waiting for. That I was worth waiting for."

He leaned in and placed a soft kissed my forehead. "And you still are."

Hot tears welled up and spilled over.

"I wish you were so moved by those words back then," he chuckled as he wiped the moisture from under my eyes.

I giggled. "I didn't talk to you for a whole week."

"Not until Christmas morning and you opened my gift."

"Makeup. I hadn't seen makeup in real life before. And you signed the card, 'to the young woman of my heart'. I instantly forgave you."

"Was it the makeup or the card that made you so forgiving?"

"A little of both," I said with a sniffle and a smile. "We never did get to kiss... well, a mutually intended kiss."

Stoyan tensed. "I was waiting for you to turn eighteen. I never wanted it to be said that I took advantage of you or coerced you in anyway. I wanted the decision of intimacy to be made by you, with the clear conscience of an adult. But that day never came—"

"Because I left when I was sixteen," I finished.

"That you did," he whispered as he turned his head.

He was angry again.

Not thinking, I placed my palm on his cheek. "I am twenty-eight now. Am I old enough for that kiss?"

What am I doing? What the hell am I doing?

Stoyan turned back to me. Even in the darkness, I could see his eyes boring into mine, his mind struggling to figure out this change in events.

Damn. I couldn't even explain it to myself. I mean, we were ex-betroths, yet married. There was just as much pain and anger between us as there was love and desire. We had a long history together, and a long list of unresolved issues. We hadn't seen each other in twelve years, but it felt as if we'd never been apart.

I slid my hand behind his head, gently pulling his face toward mine. I pressed my lips lightly against his, initiating the second kiss of my life.

Instantly, his tongue found its way past my lips. I moaned as his warm mouth assaulted mine in a frenzy of passion. He tasted so wonderful.

My heart raced as his hand slid up my pajama top and rested between my breasts. I arched up and put my arm around his back, tugging him down upon me so his large, hard body covered mine. Butterflies flapped in my stomach and moisture gathered between my thighs. I needed more of... something.

Though he was pressed against me, nothing but the fabric of his t-shirt and boxers and my pajamas between us, it was still too much distance.

He trailed kisses across my checks and down my neck, his hands moved over my breasts, caressing them.

I wanted these damn pajamas off. I wanted his skin to touch my skin. I wanted to become one with him.

Pajamas?

How in the hell did I get into my Pajamas?

Should I care?

Yes, I should.

My cheeks flamed in embarrassment and self-consciousness replaced my building desire. Stoyan must have dressed me—or undressed me and redressed me. What kind of underwear did I put on this morning? Shit, probably white granny panties.

As his fingers slid over my nipples, I realized I no longer had a bra on.

Son of a bitch.

Control your temper, Katia.

I gently nudged him up off me. Even in the shadows, I saw him look at me expectantly.

"I need to… um… take a shower," I stuttered breathlessly, knowing it sounded like the lamest excuse ever.

He nodded, and allowed me to get up.

Stoyan remained in bed as I made my way to my bathroom. Even though my back was turned, I could feel his gaze searing me, igniting my blood. My anxiety level shot up so much I heard buzzing in my ears.

Shaking, I closed the door behind me and locked it. After turning on the shower, I shucked off my pj's and climbed into the hot, streaming spray, willing the water to wash away all the confusion surging through my body.

I was an emotional mess. I was sad. I was scared. I was nervous. I was horny.

I couldn't believe I had almost had sex for the first time with a man I hadn't seen in twelve years. I mean, really. Out of nowhere, Stoyan shows up at my door and saves me from a ghost. Then with the first words out of his mouth, insults me, and worse, defends his rude remarks by claiming to be my husband via a ceremony I wasn't even present for.

And I almost slept with him?

How fucked up am I?

Shit! How could I have allowed things to go so far?

I really needed to get some control of myself. For over a decade I'd never felt the need for companionship. Hence, my state of virginity. But Stoyan comes back into my life uninvited, and I act like a cheap slut.

What if I had given him my virginity?

Then the matrimonial ceremony would've been completed.

Then he would've tried to take me away to wherever he lived and expect me to act like a wife. To love, honor and obey him.

Oh, *hell* no…

And he'd want me to bear his children, too.

I don't want children. What if they inherited my gifts?

No, I would never wish this curse of mine on someone else, especially my own flesh and blood. Stoyan and I just couldn't happen. I had to put a stop to this—to us.

I know he wouldn't listen to reason, so I'd do what I was best at, which was running away.

I had no choice. I would have to leave. And soon.

Chapter Four

After donning a bathrobe, I left the bathroom, trying to think of something to say to the man in my bed. Luckily, Fate was with me—Stoyan was asleep. I quietly tiptoed past him and made my way to the kitchen.

I about died.

The place was cleaned up! If not for the thin, clear plastic sheet covering the broken windowpanes on the French doors, it would seem that nothing had happened there at all.

I rushed into the living room next. Cleaned too!

A husband who cleans…who would have thought?

Ugh! He's not my husband.

Returning to the kitchen, I started a pot of coffee and glanced at the clock. It was three in the morning. Oh well, I'd slept enough and God knows I didn't want any more dreams.

While the coffee brewed, I carefully opened the patio doors, wincing when they creaked. I froze in place and listened. No sound from came from the bedroom.

Good.

I went out onto the deck, but didn't close the door behind me for fear the battered wood would let out another groan. The first thing I noticed, to my surprise, was the patio furniture. Wow, Stoyan had even thought of that.

It was harder to hate him when he was so thoughtful.

Rules of Darkness   *33*

Waking past the patio furniture, I approached the railing and glanced up at the clear night sky, then let out a heavy sigh when I noticed the full moon. Just another reminder of how I was not a normal person.

I swear, the bright white orb was taunting me.

How could something so beautiful be so dangerous? I followed the moon's eerie glow down to its wavering reflection on the lake's surface. I glanced around my lawn, and then let my gaze wander to the forest that surrounded my isolated haven.

When I purchased the cabin, I never thought to ask if any usual animal attacks had happened in these parts. Scanning the tree line, I tried to peer through the shadows. Was there any movement? Not that I could tell.

What were the odds of a shifter roaming somewhere in there?

Of course it was possible, since most people suffering from moon madness tended to live in out-of-the-way areas, hoping to better guard their secret. However, being that there were not many homes around here, each dwelling separated by miles of forest and dirt roads, it was unlikely that one of my remote neighbors suffered from such a rare affliction.

In the distance, a lone howl filled the crisp air, as if to disagree with my assessment.

I hugged myself to stop the chill racing up my spine. My luck couldn't be that bad, could it?

So what, I told myself. There's a wolf around, no big deal. It didn't mean it was a shifter. It could be just a normal, average, everyday wolf. Anyway, unlike the movies, shifters tended to stay in their own territory, and like real wolves, rarely made an appearance in well-lit or populated areas.

But unlike real wolves, shifters were slightly larger.

Okay, and slightly smarter, or so I was told.

And extremely aggressive.

In all my twenty-eight years, I'd never encountered one, so why would I now? Did I not flee my village the night of the full moon? Nothing happened to me then, and there was suppose to be a pack of werewolves running around in that forest. I liked to think that if I was destined to be screwed by a shifter in its wolf form, it would have happened when the odds were at their greatest.

Maybe the elders were wrong about my *scent*.

Matter of fact…where was Charlie? I hadn't seen him yet.

I whistled low, hoping that he didn't run too far from home when Stoyan ordered him out earlier.

I heard a whimpered response

I whistled again.

Another whimper followed by the sound of crackling vegetation.

My eyes were drawn to the lakeshore. Even with the moonlight, I couldn't see my dog, but the violent swaying of tall grass and overgrown reeds alerted me to his location.

"Charlie! Get out of there!" I hissed.

The rustling continued, making its way toward the old boat dock.

"Charlie! Come here!"

The hair on the back of my neck rose. The dock entrance was covered with the same flora that ran along the shore. I suddenly regretted not taking the time to clear it out.

I heard the pitter-patter of paws on wood.

"Charlie?" I called softly.

Suddenly a four-legged shadow emerged onto the dock and made its way down the path of planked wood. A chilly breeze rose, fluttering my hair and robe.

Charlie stopped, then instantly crouched low, a growl emanating from his throat. My heart leapt in my chest as another shadow materialized at the dock's end.

Oh, my God!

"Charlie!" I screamed.

Rules of Darkness
35

The shadow moved, quick as lighting, and was next to Charlie's form in an instant.

I sprinted for the deck's stairs.

"No, Katia! Stop!" I heard behind me.

I didn't care what Stoyan wanted. Charlie needed me.

Down the steps and I was off, cold damp grass under swift bare feet. A tingling sensation raced through my body. The closer I got to the lake, the more my body hummed with energy.

Charlie whelped.

I was almost there. My body was throbbing all over now. I felt a jolt, then nothing.

A strong hand wrapped itself on my upper arm and jerked me back. "Don't cross the barrier."

Another jolt and the throbbing returned.

In the distance, I heard a giant splash.

"Charlie!"

Instantly, the pale dead kid was right in front of me, his black eyes and long razor teeth just inches from my face.

With a gasp, I fell back into a hard chest. Large muscular arms wrapped around and steadied me.

"We are on the edge of the safety barrier. He cannot pass it," Stoyan whispered in my ear. "Not yet."

"Yet?" I croaked.

"The spirit grows stronger. And more so now, since he was so close to reaching you tonight. Sooner or later, he will be powerful enough to pass through."

"I thought you banished him."

"I banished him from the house and set the barrier, but he is not haunting the house, he is haunting you. I cannot banish him from a moving, living person. Once you leave the protection of the barrier, if he so chooses, he may come to you again."

Protection...Oh, Charlie...

My poor sweet friend. My only family.

Shaking with grief and fury, I pulled myself out of Stoyan's hold and confronted the kid. "You little bastard! I'll get you for this!"

The ghost stared at me blankly, seemingly unmoved by my threats or the tears sliding down my face.

Stoyan tugged on my arm. "Come, Katia. Let us go inside."

I wrenched out of his grasp. "Fuck that."

Was this my life? Why should I have to live this way? I lost the one thing I cared about. I was alone again.

"You are never alone, Katia. You have never been alone."

I spun around. "Mother fucker. You *can* read my mind."

I found out instantly that Stoyan did not appreciate being called a mother fucker. He grabbed my arm and pulled me towards the house.

"I do not like the way you speak to me. I understand that here in America, these words are acceptable. However, I know you were raised better. I am your husband and you should speak to me with some respect."

"Let go of me," I demanded.

He dragged me up the stairs. "To answer your question, no, I cannot read your mind, but yes, I can hear your heart when it speaks."

I tried to free my arm from his tight grip. "What the hell does that mean?"

He guided me to the kitchenette and nudged me down on a chair before releasing me. "It means that when you are thinking from your heart, I can hear you. If you have a random thought about what to eat for dinner, I cannot hear that."

Stoyan closed the patio door and locked it, then went to the cabinet and removed two mugs.

Friggin wonderful. Not only was he invading my life, he was also invading my thoughts. With him around, I guess I could kiss my freedom and my privacy goodbye.

Rules of Darkness 37

I'll be leaving soon anyway.

Crap! Could he hear that?

I studied my ex-betrothed. If he heard me, he showed no outward sign of it.

After setting the table with napkins, spoons, cream and sugar, he placed a cup of steaming coffee in front of me. He sat down in the chair next to mine, his own cup in hand. We didn't say anything to each other for a while.

I cried silent tears, thinking about my friend. I really missed Charlie.

Finally, Stoyan broke the silence.

"Katia, I know you feel like you are alone, but I am here. True, we will have difficult times ahead of us. There is so much we have to catch up on, so many years lost, and we will have to work hard to rebuild the trust we once had between us."

I rolled my eyes. Who cared? Why did he want to talk about it now? I was on some ghost kid's hit list and I just lost my best friend. I missed Charlie so much it was hard to breathe.

Stoyan reached over caressed my hair. "I know, love, but don't be sad. You have no reason to be. Do you trust that I tell you the truth?"

Yes...um...no.

I didn't respond. I was torn. My first instinct was to believe him, but I can't believe in my instincts anymore. Too many horrible events had happened to me in the last twenty-four hours to even think straight.

I loved Stoyan as much as I hated him. I knew that.

They say there's a thin line between love and hate, and that you have to care about someone before you can truly hate them. If you didn't care, you'd be indifferent to them. Why couldn't I be indifferent?

Stoyan placed his hand over mine. "There is something I need to tell you. About you, about me, about you being alone all these years. It is important that you know the truth. I want nothing hidden between us."

Shaking my head, I pulled my hand away. "Look, save it for another day. Actually, don't bother. There's nothing between us, nothing to work out. I know you think you're my husband, but you're not. Okay? So please, just let me grieve in peace."

Stoyan nodded and placed his coffee down. He rose from his seat.

I watched him go to the French doors and open them wide. The cool night air rushed in. Then the most usual sound came from the deck—the sound of quick thumping on wood.

A wet animal rushed into the kitchen.

"Charlie!"

I slid off my chair and dropped to my knees. Charlie leapt on top of me, licking my face and dampening my robe with water. I hugged him tight, my tears of sorrow now tears of joy.

Don't be sad. You have no reason to be. Do you trust that I tell you the truth?

I gave Stoyan an accusatory glare. Did the man get off on seeing me miserable?

"Why didn't you tell me that Charlie was still alive?"

"I could not because it would have violated one of your rules."

"What?"

"I cannot tell you the future. If not for my gifts, I, like you, would have thought your dog dead."

"Bullshit."

Stoyan raised his eyebrow. "And if I was not here? Would you have figured on your own that Charlie was alive and well before he appeared on the deck?"

I knew the answer was no, so I lashed out in another way. "It's a stupid rule. Everyone else in the world can have their future read, but I have to stumble through my life without guidance."

"You have guidance," he stated softly.

"Really? What guidance is that?" I snapped.

Rules of Darkness

"You have your rules."

"Oh yeah, the fucking rules. You can't do this, Katia. You can't do that, Katia. Never look in a dark mirror, Katia, or a spirit might possess you. Never pick up anything off the ground or there might be Djinn attached who'll steal you away. Never go into the forest at night during a full moon, or some werewolf might try to fuck you."

"Enough, Katia."

I rose to my feet. "Screw you, Stoyan. You've no idea what it's like to be me. Your life has been peachy easy."

He slammed the French doors closed. "Are you so sure?"

Charlie whimpered and left the kitchen, hightailing himself to the bedroom. As much as I wanted to follow my dog, I could feel the anger radiating off Stoyan, so I thought it best to stay. For some reason, seeing his anger cooled my own. Stoyan, as I remember him, rarely lost control.

He leveled me with a hard stare. "I was eight when the responsibility of protector was thrust upon my shoulders. I did not get a say as to whether or not I wanted to be a protector. While other kids were playing, I spent my free time locked away with the elders, strengthening my gifts and memorizing spells so I could better protect *you*. You talk about not having friends and being alone, yet if I wasn't with the elders, I was with you."

I shook my head in disagreement. "You went to college overseas. I'm sure you had friends there, or the very least a roommate. I'm sure there were parties you went to…" *and lovers that I don't want to know about.*

Stoyan gave a hallow laugh. "Oh, yes. School. Because not only did I have to meet my responsibilities to you as a protector, but had to fulfill my obligations to my father as his heir. Though we are estranged, I continue to do my duty to him. Upon his retirement two years ago, I took over my father's mining empire, his many investments, and other business ventures."

I was shocked to hear that Stoyan was estranged from his father. I couldn't imagine why. They had been so close.

I'd only met Stoyan's father, Stylianos, a few times, but the man was warm and kind. He always greeted me with a smile, a bear hug, and a gift. Though Stoyan and I were only engaged, he had always called me daughter. He was probably the closest thing I had to a father of my own.

At least, so I'd thought until the day my great-grandma died.

But I'm not bitter.

Well, not too much. Just a little.

Through the years, I had lost most of the anger that I once held against Stylianos' for his role in the betrayal of that day.

I guess time did heal wounds.

"Your mother?" I asked.

Stoyan paced the kitchen, his eyes betraying his injured feelings. "She stood with my father against me."

As I remembered her, Stoyan's mother was a sweet, wonderful woman who doted on her son.

I gently touched Stoyan's arm to halt his wandering. "What happened?"

Shaking his head, he placed his hand over mine. "It does not matter. You were right to say so earlier. We can save this for another day. What is important is here and now, and that I have found you again."

Like him, I didn't want to press the parent issue. I guess I would have to be patient.

Stoyan cupped my chin and lowered his head. "I am sorry," he murmured, his hot breath caressing my lips. "I should not have lost my temper. Do you forgive me?"

My skin grew warm and tingled in anticipation. *Would he kiss me if I said—?*

"Yes," I breathed, letting my eyes flutter close as my heart thumped wildly in my chest.

I was not disappointed.

Rules of Darkness   *41*

His lips were on mine, his tongue coaxing me to open my mouth to his, allowing him to deepen the kiss. I enjoyed his warmth, his taste. I pressed closer, moaning, my reeling senses wanting to drink more of him.

Suddenly, his arms encircled me and his hands cupped the lower part of my bottom. I flung my hands around his neck and held tight as he lifted me up, my legs automatically wrapping themselves around his hips. The world spun and I was momentarily weightless.

Stoyan placed me on the edge of the granite kitchen island, fitting himself tightly in between my knees, never once stopping the wondrous assault on my mouth. I clutched at his t-shirt, gathering the material in my fist, using it as leverage to pull him even closer. I grinded against his hardness, but it did little to ease the empty, tight feelings that built in my center.

He broke away and pulled the garment over his head. With the shirt gone, he captured my mouth again. My hands slid across his smooth muscular shoulders, his skin hot beneath my fingertips. He was so sexy, so strong, and so male.

My breath quickened and my blood surged. My body flamed.

His lips traveled down my neck as his fingers tugged at the cloth belt around my waist. The robe went slack, and his hands spread the material apart until it fell off my shoulders. My nipples instantly hardened in the cool air.

I pulled my arms out of my sleeves and tangled my fingers in Stoyan's hair. His lips made their way across my collarbone and down to the swell of my breasts.

Somewhere in the back of my mind, warning bells went off. If I allowed this to go on, if I didn't stop it now, I might lose myself forever.

Sparks shot through my body when Stoyan seized a nipple in his mouth, flicking the nub with his tongue.

"Oh, God," I gushed, arching my back.

It felt so good, so right. Perhaps being lost to him forever would not be so bad after all.

I pulled his head up and kissed him hard, rough and insistent, hoping to convey my wants and demanding that he meet my needs, to give my body what it craved.

His hands roamed lower, over my thighs. I tilted my hips up, spreading my legs wider, offering my self to him.

Stoyan's fingers found their way to my moist folds and gently encircled my small bud. My body quivered as the pleasure of his touch washed over me. But it wasn't enough. I ached for more, for something to fill that empty throbbing in my core. I pushed myself into his hand.

"Katia, we should stop," he said between kisses. "This is not how I imagined I would have you the first time."

I pushed his head to the side and began nibbling his neck. I clawed at his back trying to bring him nearer, and get his fingers closer to my weeping hole.

"Katia," he groaned.

I maneuvered one hand between us and shoved it down his boxers, grabbing a hold of his warm, thick rod and massaging it. God, he was huge.

"Katia, please. I do not want to hurt you."

"Prepare me," I panted. "Get me ready for you. Right now."

"No, not here. I will take you to the bedroom."

I nipped his neck in frustration. "I might be a virgin, but I'm not innocent." I pulled his cock out, squeezing and rubbing along its long length. "I've read a lot of naughty books. I know what I want," I whispered in his ear.

Stoyan slid his finger inside my tight hole, keeping his thumb on my clit. I gasped as I stretched open, enjoying the pleasure the filling pain brought. I rocked my body against his wrist.

"More. Give me more!"

Another finger and more pressure on my clit. I leaned into him, my pussy clenching. Stoyan suckled my breasts as his fingers moved in and out of me.

Rules of Darkness

"Yes! Stoyan!"

"You are so tight, yet so wet. You are about to come." He sucked hard on my nipple.

"Ohmygod!" I tensed, digging my nails into his shoulders as warm liquid spilled out.

"More, Katia. I want you slick and ready for me."

As if his hypnotic voice had command over my body, I screamed as another mind-blowing orgasm took me.

But he didn't stop; he kept milking me, relentless. I felt another climax building, even more powerful than the other two. My body trembled and my vision hazed over. I let go of Stoyan and leaned back, placing my palms on the hard stone surface, trying desperately to stop the oncoming orgasm.

"Do not," he growled.

I shook my head and closed my eyes tight. "I can't! I can't handle another one."

"You will give me what I ask," he responded

"Please, Stoyan, I'm begging you. I don't want to lose control of my body."

Despite my pleas, he continued, breaking down my barriers until I was swept away by my rushing senses. He brought his free hand up and began caressing my breast. I lost my breath, drowning in pleasure.

Somewhere in the smoky recesses of my mind, I realized I was moaning like a bitch in heat. I bit my bottom lip hard, not only to silence myself, but to allow the pain to ground me.

"Look at me, Katia."

I don't know why, but I opened my eyes and met Stoyan's intense gaze. He increased the speed of his ministrations and rolled my nipple between his thumb and finger. My body shuddered, an orgasm imminent.

"In this moment, I control your body," he said softly.

"No!" I willed my body to resist his powerful words and commanding touch.

"No?" He gave my nipple a sharp tug. "You will come right now."

I screamed, tumbling over the edge and plunging into a large black abyss where nothing but pleasure resided. My fall, wondrous, consuming, endless, was as awesome as it was devastating.

With no will left within me, I succumbed to the darkness, knowing for sure I'd die alone and lost, plummeting forever into oblivion.

I love you.

Suddenly, Stoyan was there, catching me.

"I love you, too," he whispered.

CHAPTER FIVE

In my dream, I was flying high through the sky, passing through billowing clouds. I soared over vast, mountain-filled lands, and skimmed over the tops of endless green forests. I began descending, finding myself above a large city. I navigated over buildings, over speeding cars and crowds of people. I went lower still until finally, my toes touched ground inside the guarded gates of a gorgeous, grand mansion house.

To my surprise, I saw my great-grandma making her way slowly up the walkway to the large front doors, a bundled baby in her arms.

Another vision?

I came up behind her just as she lifted her hand to knock. A thin older man in a crisp black suit opened the door. Suddenly, a bear of a man appeared, and practically pushed aside the suited man.

The large man was Stoyan's father, Stylianos.

"Elder Marija, you have made it!" He wrapped his arms around my great-grandma and gave her a hug. He released her and looked at the bundle in her hands. "You have brought our daughter!"

"Yes. Her name is Katia."

"Ileana! Come now! Come see the child our son will one day marry!"

Stoyan's mother, Ileana, appeared in the doorway. The beautiful woman looked small and fragile in comparison to her husband, but her bright eyes and sincere smile showed she was filled with happiness.

"Elder Marija, we are so honored to have you here," she offered softly and bowed her head.

"Yes! Yes! Most honored," Stylianos echoed. "Please, come in."

"Thank you for seeing me," my great-grandma replied as Stoyan's father took the baby in one large arm and used his other to assist my great-grandma over the threshold.

I followed close behind as they climbed three marble steps that gave way to a large foyer. Stylianos asked the suited man to summon Stoyan downstairs. The man bowed, shut the front door, and left.

Ileana led the way. "Elder Marija, We wish you would have told us of your coming. We would have sent someone to the village to pick you up," she said as Stylianos and my great-grandma followed her into the parlor.

"Remember, darling," Stylianos replied. "The elders do not bother with cars or trains. Horses, carriages, and feet. Maybe a sled if snow is on the ground, but that is all."

"Oh, yes, of course." Stoyan's mother signaled for great-grandma to sit in a large cushioned chair near the fire. Ileana and Stylianos sat nearby on a matching couch.

Stylianos took a deep breath. "Elder Marija, We are sorry for the loss of your granddaughter, Anya. I cannot imagine the pain you must be still enduring."

"It hurts, but such is the way of things. My little Anya left behind a precious gift, not only for myself, but for the world."

The couple nodded.

My great-grandma continued, looking directly at Stoyan's father, "I can never thank you enough for coming to the village after my granddaughter's attack. Anya would not eat, nor sleep, nor let any touch her. But your kindness allowed her to live her last months with us in peace and

Rules of Darkness   *47*

happiness. I know it was a great sacrifice on your part, and one you will bear the burden of for the rest of your life. I do not know how I could ever repay you."

I wondered what he had done for my mother. Would he say?

Tears welled up in Stylianos' eyes. He shook his head. "No, Elder Marija, you owe me nothing. It was my honor. And when I came to the village and you told me what you had told no other, that the child Anya carried would one day marry my son, it became more than honor. It became my duty."

He snuggled the baby closer to his chest and placed a soft kiss on her forehead. Ileana placed a hand on her husband's arm, a small show of support and comfort.

"We now have a new daughter," she said. "And one with such a rare gift. Imagine the good they will accomplish together, the gifts they will pass on to their children. Katia will have her mother's beauty, and my son will continue the legacy of the protector. There are so few protectors left."

As if on cue, eight year-old Stoyan appeared in the doorway. By the look of him, he could easily pass for twelve. He was large for his age, obviously taking after his father, but it was the way he carried himself that made him seem older. He didn't have the restless stance of a child. Even his eyes appeared wise, indicating he possessed a maturity far beyond his years.

Stylianos waved him over. "Come son, take Katia and get to know her. She is your responsibility. Soon, you will leave your mother and me to learn the ways of our people, and learn how to protect your charge."

Stoyan, in his usual quiet form, approached his father. Stylianos transferred the bundle into his son's arms. As if born with the knowledge, Stoyan cradled the child properly. Just as silently as he came, he left the room.

Stylianos took a deep breath. "In a few weeks, Stoyan will move to the town outside the village. I have already purchased a summer home, including the hiring of staff to run it. I also acquired a tutor to teach him his academics. For the next ten years, he will study with the elders. When he is seventeen, he must leave for college. When Katia reaches marriageable age, then he will return for the ceremony."

My great-grandma nodded. "Stylianos, I have come today, not only to present to you your daughter, but to ask another kindness from you, for the sake of Katia."

"Elder Marija, no matter what you ask, if it is in my power, the answer is yes. Anything for my daughter."

"That is honorable of you, but what I ask will bring much difficulty to your life where your son is concerned. But it must come to pass this way. We cannot alter the path Katia will choose, but we can ease the journey."

Dread seeped into my bones. As if feeling the same about my great-grandmother's words, apprehension reflected on Stylianos and Ileana's expressions.

"What have you seen, elder? What does the future hold for our children?" Stylianos asked.

Great-grandma gave a small smile. "As you know, we do not walk this world forever. One day, I too must depart this plane of existence."

Pain and resentment struck deep in my stomach. I remembered that horrible day all too well—the day my great-grandma died. Though I have forgiven everyone who was involved with that, recalling the memory of that day still carried some lingering negative emotions.

"Katia will not take this well," my great-grandma continued. "She is so delicate in spirit. She will not see that the other elders were trying to protect her when they will not let her see me. All she will understand is her grief and anger. In turn, she will flee from us, run from our way of life, try hard to abandon her gifts, and disappear into the world."

What? She knew I'd leave one day? There's no way.

Rules of Darkness 49

"Why can we not stop her? If your death brings her such grief, why can we not give comfort? She can come to live with us," Ileana offered.

"No, this is the path that destiny has chosen, and for good reason—a reason I cannot reveal to you in this moment for the future must not be made known to the other presence in this room."

I lost my breath when my great-grandma looked my way. It was a quick glance, almost negligible, but there all the same. I stepped back. Was she really talking about me?

Stylianos' eyes shifted around the room. "Yes, I feel the presence you speak of," he whispered tensely. "But I cannot see it directly. This is odd, for it is neither spirit nor fallen one. Perhaps we should not discuss this now. Are you not revealing the future by telling us that Katia will leave?"

"No, for what I am revealing is the past for the Katia in this room."

"She is here now? Watching us?" he whispered in awe.

My great-grandma nodded. "I can feel her presence. It is she, for the baby is not in the room with us, and this presence is older."

"I have heard of such vision quests, but never seen it in life. How are you so sure you are not revealing the future to her?"

"I have seen all in my dreams. I have seen what comes to pass to bring this vision for Katia, and I have seen why destiny has chosen the path Katia must take, and why we must not deter her. She must end up in the place she visits us from. The only way for her to get there is by leaving us all behind, including Stoyan. All we can do is smooth the path as much as possible."

Tears appeared in Ileana's eyes. "But I do not understand. Can we not just take her to that place when she needs to be there?"

"It is during this solitary journey that Katia finds herself, grows stronger in spirit, learns to trust again, and finally accepts her gifts and their consequences."

"What will she do without her protector? How will she survive against the darkness?" Ileana asked.

"This is why I am here today. When she leaves us, she will still be naive of the modern world and its dangers. She is so much like my Anya—"

"Then Stoyan must go with her. She must have her protector," Stylianos stated.

My great-grandma shook her head. "No, Stoyan must never know where she is until fate reveals it to him. His love of her would have him alter her course. Some things must be learned through experience. She will not experience what she needs to if he is always there to do his duty and stop the experience from happening."

Stylianos gave a resigned sigh, grasping his wife's hand as she wept quietly. "What do you need us to do, Elder Marija?"

I felt something akin to betrayal blooming in my heart. I knew in one second, the reason for this vision would be revealed. I also knew that I wasn't going to like what I was about to hear.

"I ask that you care for Katia when the time comes for her to leave. I would ask the elders, but they do not have the means to care for her in this way. You are younger, of the modern world; you have the resources, the means to care for her from afar, to see her safe during her long journey. She must never know as it is happening, she must never know that you are involved. And you must do this without revealing her location to your son."

* * * *

I opened my eyes to a dim room.

Son of a bitch!

Had the last twelve years of my life been a freakin lie?

Rules of Darkness

Through my haze of fury, my mind registered the bright sunlight trying to penetrate the blinds. I glanced at the windup alarm clock. It was 3:00pm.

Swinging back the covers, I jumped off the mattress and turned, searching my bed. But Stoyan wasn't lying next to me as expected.

Where the fuck was he?

I glanced around. The presumptuous bastard had moved his suitcase and toiletry bag in, but that was the only sign of him.

He wasn't in the master bathroom either, but he had to be around the house somewhere.

Tying the belt of my robe into a tighter knot, I stormed out of the bedroom, calling out for Stoyan. I wanted answers and I wanted them now. What exactly did his father do for me during my 'journey'? And what did his father do for my mother that earned my great-grandmother's gratitude?

I hit the kitchen first, but Stoyan wasn't in there. I glanced over to the dining room. He wasn't there either. I went into the living room next. Still, no Stoyan.

Charlie napped by the front door. He raised his head and glanced my way. "Go back to sleep," I ordered as I climbed the stairs to the loft.

I found the bright white art studio was as I left it the day before. I approached the large bay window and looked out, hoping to see Stoyan's ass in the backyard. Nope. I checked the bathroom I use to clean up my brushes. I went to the other side of the studio and opened the sliding glass door. I stepped out onto the balcony and scanned outside. Only peaceful forest scenery.

Frustrated, I went inside and slammed the sliding glass door with a satisfying thud. I descended the stairs and went back to the hallway. I knew he wasn't in my bedroom, so I check the main bathroom, then my library. Nothing. Once again, my protector was nowhere to be found. Go figure.

Now totally pissed off, I headed back toward the kitchen, wondering if he was in the attic or the basement. But why would he go there? He must have gone off somewhere, maybe to town or something. But for what?

Maybe he left forever? Didn't even bother with a goodbye?

No, I wouldn't be so lucky. If Stoyan had gone for good, he would've taken his suitcase.

As I passed the dining room, something silver and white and foreign drew my attention to the dining room table. It was a sheet of paper, the corner of which was slid under a laptop. I stomped over whisked the note from under the would-be paperweight.

Please forgive me for not being here when you awake. I promise to be back shortly, my love. Until then, please do not leave the protection of the barrier.

Crumbling the note in my fist, I threw it down on the floor. Who the hell did he think he was, dictating to me? If I wanted to leave, then I would damn well leave. Screw him and the friggin ghost. Matter of fact, a nice drive was just what I needed at the moment.

I turned to head to my bedroom, then spun back around and stared at the laptop. Was Stoyan out of his fucking mind? Didn't he know that laptops have fucking speakers? What kind of a protector wouldn't know not to bring items like this around me?

I picked up the nice pretty grey piece of modern technology and carried it to the kitchen. I opened the creaky French doors and rushed toward the railing, the laptop held high above my head.

Damn.

I didn't throw it…but I should have.

I took a deep breath and laid the small computer on the patio table. I'm not so immature that I'd destroy his personal belonging out of spite. No. That's not me. So what if he and his family—and my great-grandma when she was alive—had done nothing but lie to me all my life?

My mind shifted through all the memories from the past twelve years. My dumb ass never questioned what I thought to be my good fortune, especially in the beginning when I left the village.

Like the nice young couple I met the day after I fled. They picked me up off the road and offered me a ride to the city in their car. And then there was the nice man I met at the train station that paid for my ticket out of the city, even giving me extra money to see me through the next couple of days. There was the young woman I met on a train heading for the border. She informed me that I couldn't leave the country without a passport, but she just happened to know how to get one for me even though I didn't have a birth certificate or ID. I stayed with her for a whole month.

In my mind, I saw the faces of the countless "good" people that took me in as I trekked across numerous countries.

I should've known that something was up. Hell, maybe I *had* known. I might have been naive when I left the village, but during my travels I saw things, read the newspapers, I knew the world could be a horrible place. I kept telling myself that I was just blessed to encounter such great people.

Oh, and these nice people I stayed with never questioned anything. They never pried into my past. They didn't seem to notice the odd habits I kept; they never questioned why I wouldn't step into old buildings, or avoided old objects, or why I wouldn't go outside at night during a full moon. They never reacted to the strange occurrences that sometimes happened around me; never seemed surprised that I would sometimes get stalked by a lost person, even when that lost person tried to break into their house to get to me.

And my hosts never stopped me from leaving when I told them I couldn't stay any longer. They would just smile and ask me where I wanted to go. I never had any answer because I never knew exactly where to go next; I just knew I had to leave. Then they would offer me a list of people they knew here or there that I could stay with. I always ended up somewhere safe and sound.

The last person I stayed with was an ancient old man who just happened to know the local language of the area from which I hailed, but also my people's language. In the two years I stayed with him, he spent all his time teaching me English, math, and history. In the end, he hooked me up with something equivalent to a diploma, handed me a visa, and sent me off to America for college.

And I never even questioned the charitable, unknown "sponsor" who paid my tuition, my apartment, all of my expenses, gifted me with a vehicle, and so on, until I graduated.

God… I was so dumb.

Thankfully, not long after I finished school, I met a rich European art fanatic who loved my work. He pays me an exorbitant amount of money for every painting I send him.

Or is my patron just a part of the elaborate hoax that is my life?

Great, I thought. I'm probably a shitty artist and this is just Stylianos' new way of taking care of me.

Fucking wonderful.

Leaving the laptop on the deck, I went inside to get dressed.

I needed to get out of there.

Chapter Six

After I spent three hours driving aimlessly on the deserted two-lane highway that meandered through endless miles of forests, I was uncertain as to how I should proceed. After all, I had been outside Stoyan's magic barrier for all this time, but of course, as my luck runs, the ghost kid never showed up.

I was actually quite pissed off about that.

I'd been waiting for the spirit to appear in the middle of the road. I kept imagining myself swerving to avoid him and crashing into a tree. Then he'd come over to my dying body to snatch my soul, and I, with my final breath, would tell him to fuck off.

But the kid was a no-show.

Yes, I was tempting fate. Careless, reckless, foolish behavior on my part? Yeah, absolutely. But I couldn't seem to help myself. I was on a roll and had no desire to stop.

My current path took me through a little town, the road being the main attraction of the community. Like the highway, the town seemed empty.

As I reached the outskirts, an isolated cottage caught my attention, or actually, the signs in the front windows did.

I pulled my car up outside the small house with two neon signs that read, "Palm Readings Here" and "Walk-ins Welcome".

Why not go inside and get my future read?

Because it would break a rule?

Who cared anymore?

I turned off the engine, grabbed my purse, and stepped out of the SUV.

A soft breeze brushed over my skin and blew tendrils of my hair across my face. I looked up at the sky. A storm was slowly rolling in, allowing the setting sun to smear the pewter-colored clouds with deep amethyst that slowly faded into smoky sapphire.

The pale full moon was hiding somewhere behind the clouds, but that wouldn't make it any less dangerous to me once the sun was completely gone.

Oh well.

But you know, now that I thought about it, the evening was totally perfect for rule breaking mayhem. I could actually break a couple of rules simultaneously.

After I got my future read, I could ask the medium to contact the kid and find out what the hell he wanted. If he showed, then I could tell him that I can't help his ass and he needs to fuck off. If the kid didn't show, maybe a fallen one would. At this point, I had no problem telling demons to fuck off.

And if the fallen didn't show, then I could just take a nice long leisurely walk through the woods and see if a shifter came around. True, he might rape me, and kill me in the process, but at least I could tell him to fuck off too.

Maybe some good would come out of my stupidity— regardless of which entity I encountered. Maybe the kid would see I'm serious about not helping him and leave me alone. Maybe a demon would come and think I'm not worth the trouble, that there are already enough bitches in hell. And should there be a werewolf around, maybe he'd realize I'm not his type and my boobs are too small.

It's either sink or swim, I thought. I'll either persevere and come out stronger, or die. But at least, it would have been by choice. I'm more than ready to accept the consequences.

As I said before...careless, reckless, foolish behavior on my part? Yep. Perhaps a bit immature? Yep. But hey, we're all entitled to our moments. This was mine.

It's official. I'd done lost my mind.

I made my way toward the house, and then through its carved wood door.

Stepping onto a white marble floor, the door closed behind me, seemingly of its own accord. I was overwhelmed by strong floral scents: Jasmine, Rose, Sandalwood, and spices I couldn't identify.

Had I just stepped through a time warp? Or an entrance to a different dimension? Maybe ended up in an ancient Egyptian temple?

The room was massive, but there were no windows. I had seen them on the outside, but inside they were hidden somewhere behind pristine white walls that sported hieroglyphic designs fashioned from gold. Under each symbol, a large gold candelabrum stood, adorned with tall white candles. Every candle was lit, casting the room with an eerie, golden glow.

Alcoves lining the walls contained gold statues of cat-like creatures reminiscent of the Egyptian Goddess, Bastet.

Was all this real gold?

Despite the dense, almost gaudy, décor, it was the ceiling that had me in awe. Painted to look like the night sky, it appeared as if there was no ceiling at all. It went up forever, just endless.

I wished I were half the artist the person who created this mural was. The sky seemed so real; the stars twinkled against the inky background like a genuine night sky.

Did one just shoot to the east? No way.

In the middle of this exotic oasis was the waiting area, I guess. Like something out of a harem, large satin and velvet cushions rested invitingly upon a Persian rug. Small wood tables dotted the area, decorated with candles and burning incense. Interestingly enough, some of the tables had magazines; the only items present to remind me that I was still in the 21st century.

As I walked around the extravagant waiting area, I noticed the far back wall contained another engraved wooden door surrounded by matching shelves lined with oils, crystals, powders, and other mystical items. Beside the display, a table and two chairs were positioned next to an ornate chest.

A bell chimed, and a young woman wearing jeans and a peasant blouse walked out. She had an all-American, apple pie style. Nothing like I expected. I guess I was expecting an exotic robed priestess, or maybe even an old fortuneteller with a turban and a crystal ball, rather than some fresh-faced girl.

As she approached me, her smile faltered and her forehead creased. "Why are you here?"

Okay? Why did she think? Shouldn't she already know?

I shrugged. "Um, to have my future read and maybe talk to a dead person or two."

"But I'm being told that it's not allowed."

Great, she was hearing voices in her head. And even they were plotting against me.

I rolled my eyes. "Well, think of it this way. It might not be allowed, but I'm willing to pay you a lot of money to do it."

"It's dangerous. A Qareen might come, and it's not safe for you."

Oh, here we go with the fallen. "Yes, I know all about the personal demons that reside with us like evil companions, walking in and out of life and tempting us to sin until the day we die." I bobbed my head to the rhythm of my speech and watched the girl's pupils dilate.

Rules of Darkness 59

She cleared her throat, but I didn't give her a chance to speak.

"I know that as our soul departs this world, the Qareen stays behind, retaining the information it gained as a witness to our life. I also know the Qareen can be summoned via a medium as they like to pretend that they're our departed ghost to any who seek contact with our spirit. Yes, I know all this."

Great-grandma had taught me well.

"If you know it most likely won't be your family member, then why summon? A majority of souls leave this plane upon death of the body and move onto different things. It's very rare that they journey back to this place. The odds are that a Qareen will be the only one to answer the summons."

"True, but perhaps the Qareen I'm looking for can answer a question or two that I have about this kid I know."

"The Qareen don't know everything. And they tend to create a false story if they don't know the answer. Sometimes they create a false answer just because they can."

"Well, with the information I need, I'm sure a Qareen was present for and he would likely be more than happy to share the details with us. The kid in question is a spirit, but still walks this world, which means he was probably murdered or died very violently. The Qareen tend to be present for those kinds of deaths. Who knows, maybe the kid will show up and give us an answer."

"So not only might the Qareen come, but a restless spirit as well?" The medium shook her head. "No, I won't summon for you."

I exhaled loud. "Why not? I'm sure you have means to protect yourself."

The young woman gave an empty laugh. "I'm not worried about me. I'm told your spirit can be taken from your body by means other than death. If the Qareen realizes this, it will take your soul without a thought. If the unrested spirit comes, it might try to take your soul. You're not to touch the dead in any form."

"I'm not touching, just talking."

"They might touch you."

"Yeah, well, I'm willing to take that chance."

"Do you have a death wish?"

"No, not really, but I have to claim my life back. If I don't, I might as well be dead. I have to face my fears, no matter how dangerous."

The young woman signaled for me to sit down at the small table. "There are people who have a fear of heights, but they don't jump off cliffs to overcome that fear."

I smiled and made my way over to the reading area. "They do if they have a bungee cord attached to their ankle," I remarked dryly and took my seat.

She sat down across from me. "I don't know how much of a safety cord I can be for one like yourself, but I'll try my best to protect you."

At the mention of protect, Stoyan's image flashed across my mind.

The medium gathered my hand into hers, smoothing her fingers over my palm. "He's looking for you, you know— the man you're thinking of. He's been searching for a long time. He found you recently, but thinks he lost you again. He is near though, closer than you would imagine."

Wow, more mind reading. I couldn't seem to get away from it. "How do you know?"

"My guide told me."

"Is it a Qareen?"

"No, it's an ancient being from long ago. My name is Jackie by the way."

"I'm Katia."

"I know."

Of course! "So you'll read my palm, and then we contact spirits—or demons—whatever?"

Rules of Darkness

"Maybe." Jackie leaned over my hand and studied the lines. "Let's see what your future holds first. Palm reading is not as detailed as the cards, but I'd like to avoid the tarot with you since the cards are keys that open the spirit world... and your spirit is so... free."

"Whatever works."

Jackie shook her head and frowned. "I can't read your palm. I—I can't read it at all."

"What? You just—"

"No, you don't understand. My guide saw your future before I did. My guide has contacted your... um, my guide is calling him your protector. The man from your mind. He's on his way here. He's only a few miles away."

I exhaled. "So? By the time he gets here, we should be done, and I'll be gone. Just do it."

Jackie seemed to be growing very agitated.

"I can't. Your protector has blocked my gift. He uses powerful magic, old magic. My guide will not interfere. My guide refuses to say why."

Fucking Stoyan. Why couldn't he just leave me alone?

"Forget the future stuff then," I bit out. "Can you summon?"

"Who are you?" Jackie asked, dropping my hand from hers.

"What?"

Her eyes glazed over. "You must follow the rules. Don't break the rules. The rules will keep you safe. You must follow the rules, don't break the rules, the rules will keep you safe. You are special, you must follow the rules, the rules will keep you safe. Rules are not meant to be broken, not for you. You are special, you mus—"

I hit the table with my fist. "Stop it! I don't care about the fucking rules. Matter of fact, I'm about to break one right now, and then I'm going to break another."

Jackie snapped out of her trance.

I rose to my feet. "You want to know who I am? Well, I'm a woman who has gifts I'm not supposed to tell anyone about. That's one of my rules. But you know what? They're not really gifts—they're curses. I'm a healer for the lost, the people that this world labels crazy. I don't use that gift, not even when the lost come to me. I haven't used that gift since I was a teenager. I can also see unsettled spirits—ghosts that like to haunt people just to make life miserable for everyone they can because they're unhappy. And I can sometimes see the fallen, I see their shadows."

Jackie looked at me with fear in her eyes. "What have you done?"

I snatched my purse up to leave. "The second rule I'm about to break is me walking out that door into the dark night with a full moon in the sky. Maybe what your guide saw in my future was me being attacked by a werewolf on my way to my car."

There was an eerie groan and three powerful knocks. Then a sudden force of wind whirled through the room. Items on the shelf began flying off, crashing into walls.

Jackie jumped back as the reading table flipped over. The chest next to the table opened and a tarot deck popped out, scattering across the floor. The cards then took to the air, arranging into some kind of strange floating design.

Three more booming knocks radiated from the front door. The building began rumbling, shaking with the force of a minor earthquake. Some of the candelabrums toppled over, as did some of the gold statues. The walls began to crack.

I started laughing. "See, Jackie?" I hollered over the roar of speeding wind and cracking foundation. "You didn't even have to summon him. The ghost came on his own. All because of *my gifts*."

The earthquake abruptly stopped, but the wind didn't. Three more blasting knocks. I turned and made my way toward the entrance, stepping over scattered candles, pillows and other crap as I went. It was time to face my destiny and see what the hell this ghost wanted. Oh, and to tell him to fuck off.

Rules of Darkness 63

Jackie appeared before me—how, I have no idea. She was just suddenly…there. And Jackie was looking a little different. There was a glow about her. Gold.

"You will not open the door," she said. Her voice was mingled with another, stronger voice. It was a voice so powerful unto itself that it didn't need to yell to be heard above the whipping wind. Then Jackie's eyes became cat-like, the pupils slitting up.

I smirked. "So, the guide makes an appearance. That's all well and good, but I have a protector already. It's not your job."

"Stupid, stupid, selfish little girl. You only think of yourself," the guide replied.

Three more knocks accompanied by sound of cracking wood.

I shrugged. "Yeah, well, someone has to look out for number one. Anyway, God protects the innocent and the foolish. Let's just hope I fall under one of those."

"I am the one protecting the foolish girl who is innocent. The spirit would take you, but he is the least of the dangers here." The guide slowly lifted its arm and pointed behind me.

I turned to see hundreds of corporeal shadows emerging from the fissures in the walls. Moving with the consistency of thick lava, they slithered around, congealed in corners, and puddled on the floor. The shadows gathered and, like an oil-slicked tidal wave, surged forward.

Oh, my God!!!

I inhaled a sharp breath, expecting instant impact. But inches before the wave was to overtake us, it hit an invisible wall and washed back.

"Those are not Qareen," the guide continued. "Those are the masters, the original fallen. They have been told of your presence in this place, a place that is a gateway, a place that they might enter easily and without permission. A place a being with an unattached soul should not be. They have come for you."

For the first time since I woke up that afternoon, I actually felt fear. I thought for sure I would never feel fear again, or wouldn't allow myself to feel it again, but there it was, crawling through my insides. In all my life, I had never seen anything like the evil spreading itself across the reading area. I turned back to the guide, not wanting to see the demon's second attempt to break through the barrier.

The guide tilted its head, assessing me. "I alone hold them at bay. Your spirit would now be in hell if not for me, for my mercy, for my intervention. A great treasure you would be for such as them. They could feed off you for eternity and gain great power by doing so. It is rare for them to encounter a meal such as you. The souls that come their way are usually shriveled and rotten."

"They would eat me?"

"It would be an endless torment unimaginable to your kind. Your kind does not grasp the concept of *endless* in this phase of your existence, but I assure you, it would not be an experience you would want to endure for a second, much less for eternity."

Three more knocks reverberated through the room. Random objects were swept-up into the blurring whirlwind that formed around us.

The guide smiled. "You wanted to speak with the dead. You wanted to speak with demons. Is this still your wish? Should I let them pass?"

I shook my head, fear taking away my ability to speak.

"The foolish can learn wisdom." The guide clucked its tongue. "Your protector has come. He banishes the spirit."

The wind came to roaring stop. All things airborne went crashing to the floor. The door burst open.

The expression on Stoyan's face was more than angry. It was enraged. His furious gaze raked over me as he approached. He didn't say anything, just towered over me and stared me down. Then he peered over my shoulder. I glanced back to see the shadows had increased their assault on the barrier, wave by wave, crashing into it.

Rules of Darkness

He stated something quietly in the ancient magic language I didn't understand. I turned around in time to see him bow his head. The guide gave reply, looking at me with disdain. Stoyan nodded, said something else, grabbed me roughly by the arm, and dragged me out the shop.

Chapter Seven

"What did the guide say?" I asked as the severely beaten shop door closed behind us with a loud bang.

Stoyan didn't reply. He just pulled me along in utter silence into the deepening darkness toward his car. Lightening flashed in the distant skies, followed a few seconds later by a roll of thunder carried in the wind.

"I know it was about me," I pressed.

He stopped and swung around, leaning in close. "It said if I were a proper master, I would beat you for your insolence. Immediately."

Proper master?

Before I could respond, Stoyan was dragging me away again.

"Wait!" I jerked back, but was unable to loosen his tight hold on my arm. "I have to drive myself home."

Stoyan reeled me around to face the direction of where I parked. He held out his open palm.

"Rumani kal su atu."

A flash of light flew out of his hand and hit a nearby tree with a deafening crash. I cringed as the tree instantly went up in a ball of flame and illuminated the area. My SUV was brought to focus.

AHH!

Rules of Darkness   *67*

My beautiful baby was destroyed. It looked like it had been mangled with a wreaking ball. Only the doors remained recognizable.

"That fucking kid!"

Stoyan gave a sharp tug, and resumed our original course. I didn't resist, I was too shocked to protest. What use would've it been anyway? My car was completely destroyed.

Stoyan unlocked the passenger door of his car and swung it open. "Get in."

I slid into the leather seat and he slammed the door shut. I absently put on my seatbelt as he folded himself in the driver's seat. The Mercedes' tires squealed as he drove off.

Within minutes, all traces of the town were gone. We mutely drove along the dark two-lane highway toward home, the darkness occasionally interrupted by bursts of lightning from the oncoming storm. I allowed myself to be lost in the shadowy blur of passing trees, replaying the events of the last two days in my mind.

Shit. It had been an emotional rollercoaster. Fear, shock, hopelessness, shame, grief, anger, passion, indifference. And it seemed that the cycle was staring over again. I had just experienced fear and shock less than an hour earlier, and now I was feeling the heavy weight of self-pity and shame sinking in. All because I knew Stoyan was furious with me. Worse, he was disappointed.

Suddenly, my mind's need to assert my independence demanded that I tell him to get over himself, that I'm a grown woman and can do whatever the hell I want, when I want.

I didn't want to care that he was upset...but I did. I guess it was because, deep down, I knew he loved me, and it feels wrong to let down the ones who love you. And to my dismay, no matter how hard I tried to fight the feeling, I wanted to make him happy again.

"I know you're angry because I broke the rules and put myself in danger, but it was something I had to do. And yes, I know I almost got myself killed, and it was stupid to let my emotions overrule good judgment, but we all do stupid things sometimes. I'm sorry."

Silence.

"Do you hear me?

More silence.

"I said, I'm sorry."

He had to have heard that, yet still he did not respond. I gazed at him, annoyed by his continued silence. "Are you not going to accept my apology?

Nothing.

I waved my hand in the space between us. "Hello? Anyone there?"

He couldn't even bother to spare me a glance, much less an answer.

Rolling my eyes, I turned away. "Fuck you then."

I could feel his anger surge. It was a tangible presence in the air, thick and stifling, encompassing the small area inside the car.

"I don't know why you're pissed," I muttered. "If anyone should be mad, it should be me. I'm the one who went on *vision quest* and found out that I've been living a lie the last twelve years. Thanks to my great-grandma and your father. So tell me, Stoyan, what *exactly* did your father do for me and my mother?"

When he didn't reply, I closed my eyes and leaned back in the seat.

So this was my life? Was I to live in fear, never having any control over anything, following these fucking rules until the day I died? I knew I was unable to rid myself of the gifts I held, but it seemed I couldn't even ignore them anymore.

I glared at Stoyan as angry tears sprang forth. Why should I bother explaining my actions to him? Who was he anyway? My husband? Yeah, whatever. He didn't even know me—hadn't seen me in twelve years. So how would he understand how I felt? How could he when he was too caught up in his own misguided beliefs to possibly empathize with my struggle?

Ha! This man, who insisted on acting like my husband, couldn't even bother to look at me.

Nice, I thought. Glad he cared so much.

Swiping at the moisture on my cheeks, I turned away, staring back into darkness. As if ghosts, demons and werewolves weren't enough, I had to deal with this asshole too. I wished the guide had let me open the damn door.

The Mercedes came to a screeching halt.

I pitched forward, but the seatbelt held and yanked me back into my seat. "What the fuck!"

I searched the road for the cause of this sudden stop.

After slamming the gear stick into park, Stoyan jumped out of the car. A sense of foreboding formed in the pit of my stomach as I watched him storm around the front of the Mercedes, his scowl fierce in the harsh light of the high beams.

A moment later, my door was jerked open. I sat dumbfounded as he leaned over my body, unbuckled my seatbelt and pulled me out.

He dragged me to the front of the car, sat down on the hood, pulled me over his lap, and…

Whack-whack-whack.

Yes, Stoyan smacked my ass. Three friggin times.

It didn't hurt, but how humiliating? What was I? A toddler? Why would he do such a thing? Thankfully, my mind came up with a quick retort.

"Are you being the proper master beating me for my insolence?" I asked caustically.

"No, you are acting like a selfish child, so I am treating you as such. When are you going to grow up and act like the woman I know you are?"

So, he equates me to a selfish child now?

"Oh. Sorry daddy—sorry you don't like my childish attitude. Instead of spanking my ass, maybe you should just kiss it and be gone. You can kiss my ass and go to hell for all I care."

I started squirming, struggling for my release, but for the life of me, I could not get out of his grasp. I was stuck there, slung over his lap like some irate, spoiled kid fighting against their punishment.

"Fuck! I wish you'd just go to hell!"

"You should not wish such things on your husband, Katia," he replied. "Do you truly want to be alone? Without a protector?"

I stilled at his chilling words, recalling the horrible demons I had encountered earlier. Knowing what I know now, I honestly would not wish that fate on anyone. But still, the bitterness I felt caused me to lash out anyway.

"Really? I didn't know you were my husband. I thought you were my 'master'."

Stoyan suddenly released me. I scrambled to my feet and out of his reach, putting a good ten feet of distance between us.

Stoyan ran his fingers through his hair. "You scare me, Katia. Your thoughts, your actions. Does your life really mean so little to you?"

There was a flash of lightening and a roll of thunder. As if the very heavens knew my grief, it started to pour. I glanced up into the darkened sky, allowing the cold water to hit my hot cheeks and hide my tears.

I fought to keep my voice steady. "I don't know if I can live this way anymore, Stoyan. The rules, the ghosts, the fallen, the lies...everything. I'm sick of living in fear. I'm not happy. I don't think I can ever be happy in this existence."

"Katia, you *can* be happy, we can be happy. But you have to let me in. Just give us a chance."

I closed my eyes and shook my head. "I don't want a master. I have enough things around me dictating my actions and ruling my life."

Stoyan let out a heavy breath. "I am not your master, not in the way you keep using it. Over 5000 years ago, back when the guide was worshipped as a god of this world, protector, master, husband—these words were interchangeable in the ancient language we were speaking. When you asked me what it said, I was angry, translating in anger. I should have chosen my words more prudently."

Stoyan pushed away from the hood of the Mercedes. He was soaked through and through. His shirt stuck to his skin, outlining his muscular chest, his hair dripping. He slowly approached, looking ethereal in the dispersed glow of headlights and mist of splattering rain.

"Forgive me for hurting you with my carelessness," he said, his deep melodic voice caressing my heart, making me want to run into his arms.

I resisted the urge to go to him. This was not like the incident with Charlie in the kitchen; he would not win me over so easily.

I held out my hand. "Don't."

He stopped. Biting his lower lip, he cocked his head and stared at the ground. I backed up a few steps. Stoyan was not in arms reach, but was still too close for my comfort.

"What can I do to make us better?" he asked so quietly, I barely heard him over the hum of the car's engine and water pounding on pavement.

I was about to answer when a sharp howl pierced the air. My breath caught in my throat and my heart near leapt out of my chest. The sound was close...very, very close.

Behind me, the crunching of bushes being crushed beneath a heavy weight filled my ears. I swung around, desperately searching the forest-lined highway. Nearby in the darkness, heavy breathing and growling marred the pitter-patter of rain.

"For the love of God, Katia, do not move and do not make a sound," Stoyan pleaded softly.

Fear held me immobilized, allowing me to comply with his request. I felt Stoyan come up behind me, and then heard the unmistakable sound of a zipper being drawn. Moments later, a warm liquid was running down my calves and into my shoes. He then urinated on the ground around me. The stream stopped and the zipper was fastened.

Oh, my God.

As if knowing that I would ask why he peed on me, Stoyan offered a whispered explanation. "It is a way of marking territory."

Even as the growling became louder, and utterly terrifying, Stoyan turned me towards him and gathered me in his arms. He placed his hands on the side of my face and stroked my hair back with his palms, as if petting me. He leaned in close, nuzzling my ears and neck with his lips.

I heard the sound of breaking twigs and the thump-thump of paws on cement. I knew the shifter was behind me before I heard the low growl emanate from its throat.

"He challenges me for the right to mate with you. When we fight, you run for the car. I will hold him back until you can drive away. Promise me you will do this."

"I can't leave you.

He brushed his mouth against mine, and then proceeded to lick my cheeks, marking me with more of his 'scent'.

"Please do as I ask," he whispered.

The growling became louder, more aggressive.

Not wanting him to be distracted with worrying over me, I nodded. "Okay."

"I love you, Katia."

"I love yo—"

I was pushed to the side. I landed on the ground, scraping my knees on the rough roadway.

I twisted back to see the wolf was on Stoyan. Suddenly, Stoyan's body began morphing, his clothes

Rules of Darkness

literally coming apart at the seams. I sat frozen, horrified, watching his body change into a huge beast.

Once transformed, Stoyan rolled the other shifter off him. The creatures circled each other, the pouring rain and rolling thunder unable to cover the primitive growls of warning. Large, fierce fangs shined in the headlights, both sets of eyes possessing a feral gleam.

The challenging wolf lurched forward. Stoyan met him head on. A ferocious fight ensued, with snapping jaws and swiping claws. The savage sounds of battle filled my ears. Amidst the vicious snarls and wild shrieks, my eyelids grew heavy and everything went black.

CHAPTER EIGHT

I was back in the village, watching my fifteen year-old self stare mutely at the ground as my great-grandmother conversed with a local farmer.

"Elder Marija, you know I would give you anything you asked for. Anything I have is yours. Your people have been kind to my family, saving my young son's life when he was struck with fever, helping my eldest son with his…moon sickness…"

The farmer rubbed his jaw, his discomfort apparent.

"I would not have come if this was not the third time I have caught your great-granddaughter taking animals off my farm. I swear to you, if it had been just about my animals, I would have approached you the first time I caught her."

"I am grateful you have come today. I wish you had told me of her thievery the first time it happened," my great-grandma replied, her voiced laced with shame.

The farmer shook his head. "Elder Marija, I am not concerned about the pigs or turkeys taken. That is why, even after I caught Katia, I let her bring the animals home. I know your people rely heavily on the forest for food, and game has been scarce with the overly dry summer and harsh winter this year."

"Please do not make excuses for her actions."

Rules of Darkness

The farmer looked away. "I also know your people are proud, and even if I offered, would not have taken the animals as a gift from me. Your people have always been honorable, only accepting fair trade for services rendered. But these days, your numbers have dwindled and your young people have left you. They are no longer here to help out on the farms and to support the village like in the days of my father, my grandfather, and back through the generations."

Great-grandmother simply nodded.

The farmer pressed on, "I only came because I fear for Katia's safety. The other farms she has visited, the owners are new, unfamiliar with the ways of your people. They are not so understanding. They know someone is stealing from them. I worry she will one day be caught by them and suffer greatly…be arrested or worse.

"I will deal with my great-granddaughter accordingly, as befitting the laws of my people. She will not steal from you or anyone else again."

"Please do not punish Katia. I was hoping I could gain your permission to have her work for me, as her mother once did. I am sure I can find some task on the farm befitting a young lady her age. Having only sons, my wife greatly misses having a young girl around to dote on, and she often speaks of your granddaughter. It broke her heart when Anya passed away."

My great-grandma gave a soft smile. "I am humbled by your offer, more so knowing Katia's transgressions. But Katia is not allowed to leave the area around the village, though it seems she has been wandering far without my knowledge. My great-granddaughter is special to our people, and must stay near for her own safety. But I will always remember the kindness you showed my young Anya, and just know that my granddaughter loved you and your wife as a child loves their parents. And she loved your sons like brothers."

The farmer's expression turned solemn. "I understand, Elder Marija. If you should change your mind, the offer is always open." He bowed his head, gave young Katia a regretful look, mumbled a 'good day', and then made his way back to his horse.

When the farmer departed, my great-grandma turned and smacked my young self in the face. "You have shamed me beyond words. Go inside and wait until I call you out."

As I watched fifteen year-old Katia trudge into the shack that was her home, guilty tears streaming from her eyes, I tried to remember what I was thinking at that moment.

I remember being scared at what punishment would come my way. I also remember being angry for getting myself caught again. The situation the elders put us in, instilling this stringent sense of honor and pride, not allowing us to accept help or gifts from outsiders, was simply too much for a child to deal with.

The food had been meager for months, and the elders often went without in order for the remainder of the village to be sustained. The elders always managed to find a small rabbit and some potatoes so that I would have a nutritious meal.

I also believed if we had more food, my great-grandma would not be so weak and sickly, plagued by a cough that only seemed to get better when she had adequate, healthy food to eat.

Once young Katia was in the house, I followed my great-grandma to Hammu's home. When she knocked on the door, he came out, Stoyan following close behind.

"Elder Hammu. My great-granddaughter has acted shamefully, and broke the laws of our people. She is to be punished. As she has no father other than Stylianos, who is not here, her punishment falls to you as the closest father-like male to her."

Hammu blinked, obviously shocked. "What has she done?"

Rules of Darkness 77

My great-grandma explained all that the farmer had said.

"Marija, you would have me bring a whip down upon your great-granddaughter's back? Please, do not ask this of me."

My great-grandma nodded, moisture gathering in her eyes. "Yes, it is our way. She must learn. She is a young girl, so three lashes is all our law requires for her."

"As an elder of the village, you have the authority to proclaim punishment. This is a most severe penalty for theft. Surely, a lesser punishment would suffice.

"If you will not do it, then I will ask another," she replied.

Stoyan stepped up, his shoulders squared and his head held high. "I will take her punishment."

My great-grandma shook her head. "It is not allowed. Only her husband can take her punishment. Though you are my great-grandson, the marriage ceremony has not taken place."

"I am her protector. By law, it is allowed. You know this to be true, Elder Marija. Yet, you would try to deny me? I respectfully ask you why?"

Tears poured from great-grandma's eyes. "Oh, Stoyan. Will you always be so kind? Will you always stand by her when her foolish behavior brings dire consequences? Will you always protect and defend Katia as you do in this moment, no matter what fate brings between you two?"

Stoyan fell to his knees and bowed his head. "Yes, Elder Marija. I love her. I will care for her and protect her always. I will give my life for hers if I must. I swear this to you, great-grandmother."

Holy shit!

My great-grandma placed her hand on his head and gave him her blessing.

I about died. For one, Stoyan's declaration reminded me of some oath-spouting knight from my historical romance novels. Two, I never knew the penalty for stealing was so harsh. My great-grandma never said, she just told me that Stoyan took my punishment. Three lashes? With a whip? Damn, I had just assumed he got paddled like I usually did for the other child-like offenses I committed.

Stoyan rose to his feet and followed Hammu and my great-grandma to the small stable. As Stoyan removed his shirt, Hammu retrieved the whip.

My great-grandma spoke. "I will get Katia now, so she may witness the pain you bear for her."

Stoyan lifted his arms and allowed Hammu to tie his hands to a wood post. "Please, Elder Marija, I would not have her see this. I do not wish to have her upset. In many ways, she is still a child. I am sure she did not understand the consequences of her actions. In her heart, she must have had good reason for doing what she did."

"It is true that my Katia lets her heart rule her actions. But without this lesson, how will she ever grow to learn about consequences and taking responsibility for ones actions?"

"If, and when, the need arises, Elder Marija, I vow to guide her and stand beside her."

My great-grandma let out a heavy breath. "I will honor your request, but I fear, one day in the future, you and Katia might come to regret this decision."

Hammu stepped back and unfurled the leather coil. "I will try not to leave scars, but I would be lying if I said this would not hurt.

Stoyan nodded.

I closed my eyes, but the sound of the cracking whip tore through me all the same.

* * * *

I opened my eyes in time to see lightening piercing the sky. I squinted through the pouring rain, trying to remember where I was.

Stoyan!

I shot up and saw his naked body lying on the road only a few feet away. There was blood everywhere.

Rules of Darkness

"Stoyan!"

I crawled over to him. The storm raged on, the rain blinding, my hair falling into my eyes, my shoes slipping on the waterlogged road, and my clothes soaked and tangling around me like a sodden straight jacket.

Stoyan's skin was cold to the touch, but he was still breathing. Water diluted the blood that oozed from the many wounds covering his body.

"Stoyan! Wake up! Wake up!"

No response.

What could I do? I didn't own a cell phone, which left me unable to call 911. But I had to get him to the hospital. He was bleeding to death before my eyes.

Grabbing his arms, I tried lifting him up, praying that adrenaline would give me the strength I needed to get him off the ground and into the car. But he was too heavy.

It could be hours before someone drove down this highway, and I couldn't leave him in the cold rain to wait. If I had a blanket, I could roll him on it and pull him to the car.

I ran to the Mercedes, and popped the trunk. It was empty. No blanket, no first aid kit.

I sprinted back. I would have to drag him across the pavement.

I maneuvered his arms above his head and started to tug with all my might. I'd moved him maybe two inches when my fingers slipped and I fell back, landing on my ass hard enough to rattle my teeth.

Back on my feet, I tried again. But no matter how hard I worked, I could not get a good grip on his slick skin. I could not get him to move.

Screaming in frustration, I collapsed on the ground, sobbing pitifully. "Stoyan, please wake up. I can't do this. I can't save you. Just wake up," I pleaded.

All of this was my fault. For so many years, I had been so caught up in my own pain; I never saw the impact my actions had on others.

Had I always been so blind? Had I been this selfish my whole life?

I failed Stoyan tonight, as I did twelve years ago. Even though I loved him, I couldn't find the courage to trust in him, even when he had done nothing but right by me. And here he was, dying in my arms, dying because of me, dying because he tried to protect me. Once more, he suffered the dire consequences of my foolish behavior.

If I had just followed the rules, none of this would've happened.

God, how many people have I let down in my life? Perhaps all those times I'd refused to use my gift? Refusing to heal the lost that had come to me? How many people in my life had died because I wouldn't acknowledge my gift?

Even on this night, my irresponsibility knew no bounds. Poor Jackie. What if her guide had not been powerful enough to stop the onslaught of the fallen? What if they had not only killed me, but had killed her as well?

Tears streamed in a torrent down my cheeks. I cried harder than I had ever cried before. I moved to his side and bent over him, laying my head on his chest.

"Stoyan, don't die on me. Don't leave me in this world alone…I need you."

A hand brushed against my head. "I am here, my love."

I rose up, my hands grasping his shoulders. "Stoyan, Stoyan! I'm sorry—sorry—this is my fault—must get you to the hospital. I should've just—if I would've liste—"

"Shh, Katia. I am well. No hospital… need… rest… home in bed. No more. Do not cry." His eyes fluttered closed again.

No!

I tugged on his arm. "Don't go back to sleep! You have to get up. I will not stop crying until your up and in the car."

He didn't respond.

I started shaking him. "Get up! Damn it, I love you! If you love me, if you've ever loved me, you'll get up right now!"

Chapter Nine

By the time I turned into my driveway, the inside of the car was steamy. I had the heater on full blast the whole ride home, wanting to banish the chill that shook Stoyan's body when we first got on the road.

Putting the Mercedes in park, I turned off the engine and glanced over at Stoyan. Sleeping in the passenger seat, he looked peaceful, almost boyish. I hated the thought of waking him up.

Leaning over, I softly caressed his cheek, pleased to find him warm, but not feverish. His color was returning to normal, and miraculously, his wounds had healed some.

Was this why he didn't want me to take him to the hospital? Because he heals so fast? Was this what it was to be a shifter?

At first, I almost took him to the emergency room, despite his request not to go. I thought he was trying to protect me, hospitals being unsettled places by nature, full of dying people and restless spirits. But after he helped me lead him off the road and into the car, he had made me promise to go straight home.

I wanted to trust him. I wanted to keep my promise to him. I wanted to be a good wife. So, against my better judgment, I did as he asked.

"Stoyan? Wake up, honey. We're home."

He slowly opened his eyes. "Thank you for listening to me."

I nodded. "You're healing quickly. Is this because you are a shifter? A werewolf?"

"Not a werewolf. I can shift shape…with magic."

I frowned. "Why didn't you use magic to kill the other shifter? Why did you fight him to the death?"

Stoyan shook his head. "Not to the death, did not want to kill him…the wolf is still a human. I fought to win you, to make him leave the area."

Figuring that all this talking was probably using up energy he needed for healing, I ended the discussion and exited the car. I would have to wait until later to satisfy my curiosity.

Helping Stoyan out, I walked him into the house and straight to the bedroom.

Guiding him into the bed, I covered him with the comforter and turned off the light. Sitting by his side, I lightly stroked his hair until his steady breathing assured me he was asleep again.

I was exhausted. I wanted so much to curl up next to Stoyan and join him in blissful slumber, but before I could, there was a matter of hygiene to attend to. After all, aside from the blood, I had been peed on.

I headed for the bathroom for a much-needed shower.

After my shower, I put on my robe and went to check on Stoyan again. I placed my hand under the comforter, laying my palm over his heart. The beat was strong and steady, and his chest rose and fell with even breaths. I let out a soft sigh of relief. He was alive and well, still sleeping… naked… in my bed.

Stoyan. My husband. The man I love.

Naked.

Alone.

In my bed.

The prospect of lying down got so much better.

However, instead of crawling under the blankets right then, which is what any sane woman would have at such a moment, I left the bedroom and went into the kitchen to make a cup of hot chocolate.

I may have been dead tired, but I never go to bed with wet hair. I hated sleeping on a damp pillow. Usually, I would use the blow dryer, but I didn't want to risk waking Stoyan up.

While waiting for the water to boil, Charlie made an appearance. After looking out the back door to make sure there was no ghost kid hanging around, I let Charlie out to go potty.

"Don't wander too far," I whispered, closing and relocking the door.

With the cocoa in hand, I headed to the library to search for a good novel to read, something to occupy my time until my hair dried.

Flipping on my reading lamp, my fingers roamed over the bindings of my favorite books. *Silencing Sarah, The Curse, Lady in White, The Last Celtic Witch...*

"Ah, here we go." I pulled *Eyes of the Dead* off the bookshelf and settled into the comfy loveseat.

* * * *

Someone was in the room with me. Even in my deep, dreamless sleep, I could feel his presence.

It was Stoyan. I knew it before I opened my eyes.

He stood before my bookshelf, wearing only a short towel around his waist. Freshly showered, his hair was slicked back and his skin glittered with moisture. Damn, he looked yummy, like something off the cover of a magazine.

As he scanned over the books, I noticed that all the scratches and bites on his skin had faded into nothing but faint red marks.

Could we make things work between us? Could we really have a life together?

"I'm glad to see you're feeling better," I said.

Stoyan turned and smiled. "I am. Thank you. I apologize if I woke you."

I shook my head slightly. "No, no, it's fine. I guess I fell asleep reading."

"I know. I checked on you earlier, before I took a shower."

"Um, your wounds are almost completely healed. Since you were bitten by a shifter, does that mean you'll turn into a werewolf next month?"

Shit! Could I have been more blunt?

Thankfully, Stoyan didn't seem offended or worried. "Protectors are not able to get the moon madness. I believe it is something in our blood, a benefit of our gift. So no, I will not change."

"Oh, that's good."

He pulled *A Werewolf Named Bunny* off the shelf. He smiled, his eyebrow rising in silent question.

I bit my bottom lip. "The werewolf in that book is nothing like the werewolves we know."

Stoyan put *A Werewolf Named Bunny* back and pulled out *Vampires 101*. Turning the book over, he read the description, then rolled his eyes.

I giggled. His expression was too much. It was that manly 'how can you women read this romance stuff?' look.

"This has an interesting title," he remarked as he took *Wish Me Up, Rub Me Down* off the shelf.

"That's a story about two Djinn and one lucky woman," I explained, laughing and blushing at the same time.

"Really?" Stoyan opened the book and scanned one of the pages.

He must have stumbled onto one of the hotter scenes, because his eyes grew wide. Then, he looked over at me like I'd grown two heads.

I was laughing so hard I could barley breathe. "What?" I asked innocently. "I told you I read naughty books."

"A virgin, but not innocent...yes, I remember," he said slowly, his gaze turning heated.

I felt my cheeks burn as I recalled the exact moment I told him such a thing. My laughter subsided as moisture pooled between my legs. I bit my bottom lip to quell my whimper and pressed my thighs tightly together, hoping to hide the desire building inside me.

Stoyan returned *Wish Me Up, Rub Me Down* to the bookshelf. "Tell me about the book you're reading."

I swallowed hard, looking down at the book in my lap. "You want to know about *Eyes of the Dead*?"

Why did he want to know?

My heart thumped wildly as I watched him approach the couch. My stomach somersaulted when he sat down next to me, leaving no space between us.

"Yes," he replied, his voice deep, husky.

It took a moment for my thoughts to collect. After all, I had a man, whose towel had stretched open to expose his muscular thighs, sitting next to me. And here I was, aroused, with nothing but a robe to shield my wet pussy.

"It's a story about a man named Antonio and a woman named Tiffany who falls in love during an adventure through the Mayan jungle."

He gently feathered the sensitive skin around my ear and neck with his finger. "Why do you like this book?"

God, he was driving me to distraction. Goosebumps formed on my skin. "Um, I guess because Tiffany and I have a lot in common," I whispered.

"Like what?"

Like we both made it through college without losing our virginity.

Well, kind of. At least Tiffany ends up losing hers in passionate scene that left me hot and bothered on many occasions. Yet, I was still untouched...but then again, maybe not for long.

"Katia?"

"Oh, sorry. Um, I don't know," I lied.

Rules of Darkness

It was too hard to think of another answer when I was getting lost in the sensations of his touch. His caress trailed the 'V' of my robe to the swell of my breast. My breath faltered and my skin tingled in anticipation.

"Hmmm. I do not know if I believe you." A devilish smirk graced his features. "What of the hero?"

Stoyan's finger slipped in-between the robe's layered fabric, sliding down to where it was held together by the belt. He gently tugged on the knot and released it.

God, the knot was undone, but my robe still folded over my body like a damn cloth chastity device.

"Katia, are you going to tell me about the hero?"

"Um, Antonio's awesome...brave, sexy..." *he's very much like you...*

Fuck! I just wanted him to rip the robe right off.

Stoyan chuckled.

Damn, he must have heard my thoughts.

He gestured to the book in my lap. "Read your favorite scene to me."

What?

"How about the page you have folded? It seems you read that page often," he said.

Oh, God, no. Not that scene!

When I didn't move, Stoyan picked up the book and placed in my hands. "Read for me, Katia," he whispered in my ear.

Trembling, I opened it to the marked page.

"*Lowering his head again, Antonio continued to ravish Tiffany's eager body with his lips and tongue—down from her collarbone, to the valley between her breasts, then slowing his descent and building her agony for release. His hand cupped her left breast as his head moved to the right. Tormenting her with each tiny lick, he took his time closing his lips and suckling her straining peaks.*"

Just as the book described, Stoyan's lips were on my neck while his fingers simultaneously opened my robe, spreading the material across the cushions. His large hand grasped my breast, kneading and massaging the tender area. My body trembled and the ache within intensified.

His kisses traveled from my neck to my chest, moving torturously slow the further down he went. I found myself moaning, arching my back, wanting more, wanting to give more to his skillful hands.

I gasped when his mouth closed over a firm nipple as his thumb brushed over the other.

"Keep reading," Stoyan gently demanded.

Shit! Where was I? I scanned the paragraphs trying to find my place. Unsuccessful, I just picked a random spot to read from.

"*Antonio's tongue swirled in her belly button as his fingers fueled the fire burning within her.*"

Stoyan slowly made his way down my body, his lips and hands wandered past my stomach, over the curls on my mound, and down the length of my thighs until he was off the couch and on his knees before my trembling body.

"Open for me, Katia," he whispered.

Oh. My. God! Did Stoyan know what happened next in the story?

As if caught up in some erotic dream, I found myself spreading my trembling legs

"Katia, I did not say to stop reading," he admonished gently as his large hands cupped my ass and guided me to the edge of the seat. Spots formed in front of my eyes as he rubbed my aching sex.

I took a deep breath. "*Tiffany's moist folds...*"

Stoyan plunged a finger into my dripping hole. As he stroked my inner desire, coaxing more cream from my center, his other hand returned to my breast, rolling and tugging on the sensitive nipple.

Oh, God, I was going to come. Hard.

"Katia," he warned.

"I-I can't read anymore. Please," I begged.

"Read. Now."

It took all my concentration to continue.

"Tiffany's moist folds spread for him and he found her tiny nub, magnifying the sensual ecstasy."

With a slight dipping of his head, his tongue began lavishing my clit, lapping and nipping the swollen bud until my whole body shook.

I was going to die!

"Her body reacted and drenched his fingers."

I screamed, my body exploding in a supernova climax.

As my body shook in orgasmic aftershocks, I tried to focus on the blurring words crossing the pages.

Stoyan swatted the book from my hands. "I can take it from here, my love."

He lifted me into his embrace and carried me down the hall to the bedroom. Kicking open the door, he gently placed me on the bed, and covered my body with his

Capturing my lips, his hard cock found my entrance. In one smooth glide, he sank in, breaking the delicate tissue that represented my virginity. I inhaled sharply as my channel stretched to accommodate the intrusion.

"I love you, Katia."

I nodded, not able to find my voice. *I love you, too.*

He moved in and out of me ever so slowly, smothering my neck and chest with his kisses. His mouth seized a nipple and suckled, sending currents of electricity throughout my body. Soon, the painfully sweet throbbing in my pussy became a pleasant sensation that had me lifting my legs higher, my body wanting more of him inside me.

His rhythm turned faster, his strokes, harder, deeper. I breathlessly begged for more as my pussy clenched around his rod.

"God, Stoyan! Yes! I love you!"

Stoyan threw back his head and joined me in an erotic release, spilling his seed deep within me.

Chapter Ten

Watching sixteen-year-old Katia fight against the man who stopped her from entering great-grandma's home brought tears to my eyes.

"Let me go! I want to see her!" young Katia pleaded, her arms flailing in grief and fury.

"You cannot, Katia," Hammu replied, his arms wrapped securely around her stomach, holding her back.

Roxelana and Stoyan's mother, Ileana, stood blocking the door, both sobbing.

"I cannot let her die alone!" Katia shrieked, clawing at the hands that held her prisoner. She then kicked backwards into Hammu's shins.

I was amazed that old elder was able to hold on to my younger self. He was taking quite a beating.

"Safira is with her, and so is Stylianos. She is not alone," he contended.

"I do not care! I will never forgive you for this! Never! I hate you. I hate you all!"

The door opened and the ladies turned toward Stylianos.

I was too upset back then to care, but knowing what I did now from the other visions, I was sure they had something to do with what I was about to find out on this quest.

Stylianos looked at the ground, tears glistening on his cheeks.

Everyone knew then. My great-grandma was gone.

Katia let out an ear-piercing, heart-wrenching cry. Pulling out of Hammu's hold, she ran toward the door at full speed, and plowed into Stylianos' chest.

The large man didn't budge; he just wrapped his arms around her and held on to her tight.

"No! No!" Katia screamed. "Let me go to her!"

"I am sorry, daughter. I cannot let you. You must not touch her. I know that is your intention."

"Why should I not? Her spirit is gone! She cannot remove my soul!"

"If you touch her, your soul will flee into the spirit world as if it were you who was dead. We might not find your soul. Then you would be lost to all of us."

Katia broke down, sobbing uncontrollably. Stylianos held her close, stroking her hair as she cried into his chest.

As I watched the father attempt to comfort my child self, I heard the son's footsteps come up behind my adult self.

"I am sorry I was not there for you when you needed me," Stoyan whispered.

"It's not your fault. I know you would've been there if you could," I replied, my voice cracking. I swiped the moisture off my cheeks. "It's just one of those things. I realize that now."

Stoyan pulled me into his arms.

Unlike the vision with my mother giving birth to me, this scene was a memory that had been with me for many years. And though sometimes I still cried when I thought of this day, for the most part, I had come to terms with it.

"I'm okay, really," I said, guiding his arms tighter around me. "How long have you been here?"

He placed a kiss on the top of my head. "Long enough to watch my young betrothed kick the knees of an elder."

A small smile came to my lips. "I know, poor Hammu. When I see him again, I'll have to apologize."

Stoyan let out a heavy breath. "I am sorry, Katia. Hammu left our world six years ago."

New tears formed as I remembered the last words I said to the elder. How could I have been so cruel to a man who was like an uncle to me? I loved him very much, and now he would never know. I could not bear to have any more regrets in my life.

"You were young, Katia.

"I know."

"Hammu knew you did not mean what you said. He knew you loved him, and he loved you as well."

"I hope so."

Stoyan nudged me back and looked into my eyes. "I know so. He was my mentor. We never fell out of touch. We discussed you often."

I nodded, believing him, and felt a little better. "Is there anyone left in the village?"

"The village is not as you remember it, Katia."

"What is it like?"

"A retreat," he replied.

What? "I'm sorry? I don't think I heard you right."

Stoyan shook his head and pointed behind me. Knowing I would have to wait for that explanation, I turned around.

"Why…" young Katia wailed, "Why did she not tell me? How—how could she leave me and not say goodbye."

"She did, daughter. She left you a letter. But I know, even as she departed this world, her mind and heart was with you. She loves you so much. She did not tell you she was leaving because she wanted you to be safe."

Sixteen year-old Katia pulled back. "Where is it?"

At Stylianos' nod, Ileana approached and handed it over.

I watched my younger self open the letter and read it, knowing what was going to happen once Katia finished it.

Rules of Darkness   *93*

All these years later, I still had that letter. I would read it from time to time, as it reminded me of how I came to lead the life I do now.

Because it was after reading that letter the first time that I had decided to run away.

Besides telling me that she loved me, would miss me, and how proud she was of me, my great-grandma also explained why she didn't tell me she was dying. She also wrote that I needed to remember the importance of my gift to the world and to *always* follow the rules.

And it was because of the rules that I couldn't be with my great-grandma when she died.

Katia finished the letter and ran off into the woods.

"Should we go find her?" Ileana asked

"No, let her go and grieve. She will not try to leave until tonight. We have much to do before then."

I looked at Stoyan. "Did you know they were going to let me leave?"

His face grew dark. "Not until years later."

Well, I guess I wasn't the only one who was lied to. This must have been the reason for the rift between him and his parents.

Suddenly, the world around us turned hazy. When the vision came back into focus, it was nightfall, and we were now standing in my great-grandma's home.

Young Katia stumbled through the door, her eyes red and swollen.

"I had just returned from the funeral," I whispered to Stoyan.

Young Katia grabbed a piece of paper and pen.

I knew exactly what she was going to write.

I looked at the ground, ashamed to meet Stoyan's eyes.

"I'm sorry," I whispered. "You were right. I should have waited for you. I know that now. But please understand, at the time, I was so heartbroken and angry at the world, I wasn't thinking straight."

"I know, my love. When I found you two days ago, I was angry and said things to you I should not have. I apologize."

Young Katia folded the letter and placed a kiss on the seam. Then she got up and started gathering her belongings.

I turned to Stoyan and shook my head. "You know, I'm lucky to be alive. I traveled through the forest on the night of a full moon and made it safely to town without encountering a shifter."

"Do you remember asking me what my father did to help you? And what he did for your mother?"

I nodded, not liking the weird emptiness his voice carried.

Just as Katia was about to leave, Stylianos strolled in, muttering something under his breath.

Wait. It didn't happen like this.

Young Katia stopped in her tracks, staring off into space.

Ileana appeared behind her husband. "Your brother and his wife are here."

Stylianos took Katia's hand and led her out into the night.

* * * *

I opened my eyes and stared into the dark room.

"What was I? Hypnotized? Did your father hypnotize me?"

Stoyan pulled me closer to him. "You can say that. My father has the ability to alter memories."

"Is that what he did for my mother?"

"Yes."

"But there is a price to be paid for that gift?"

"The person who takes the memory must also bear it as if it is their own, in its true form."

So his father had the memory of my mother being raped as if he was there and it had happened to him.

"Why do all these gifts have such a terrible price attached to them?"

"It is the way the universe balances out. It stops those who have gifts from abusing them, from playing God."

"So, what really happened the night I left?"

"My uncle and aunt took you to town. In the morning, you were made to believe you were picked up from the side of the road and that my aunt and uncle were just random strangers."

"You told me that I've never been alone."

"Through the years you traveled from place to place, you were always with family or friends, people who knew about your gifts, and knew how to protect you if you needed it. My father supported you, and still does. He has your artwork hanging in his house."

So I had been living a lie...

"Then why did it take you so long to find me?"

I felt Stoyan tense up. "For years, I was led to believe that no one knew your location. I tired everything I could to find you. My magic produced nothing. Refusing to give up, I hired agency after agency to track you down. Every moment I could, I searched for you physically. But it was as if you fell off the face of the earth...no one could locate you. I never understood that, since you left as a minor, with no knowledge of the outside world, no passport, nothing."

"Why didn't you think me dead?"

Stoyan put his hand over my heart. "Because I could still feel you."

I smiled and placed my hand over his.

Stoyan continued, his voice taking on a rough edge. "About five years ago, one of the trackers grew a conscience and told me that my father had been paying him not to find you. When I confronted my father, he finally told me the truth of your disappearance. He explained what your great-grandmother had predicted and her request for his help. He confessed to blocking my magic so I could not find you. He admitted to paying off every investigator I had ever hired so they would not search for you."

This all sounded like some espionage movie. "What did you do?"

"I demanded he tell me your location. He refused."

"And you two have not spoken since."

"He continued to thwart my search."

"So how did you end up finding me?"

"A simple accident. The last painting you shipped was lost in the mail. It was only found recently, just last week. Instead of delivering it to my father's home, it was delivered to the company headquarters. Since taking over the company, anything addressed to my father is directly forwarded on to his residence by our mail department. Somehow, your painting was not. It ended up in my office, on my desk."

"Are you going to make amends with your father?"

My question was met with silence.

I pressed on, "Darling, these last two days have shown me how short life is and—"

"Exactly, and because of my father, I have lost twelve years with you. He should have never let you leave," Stoyan spat.

"But—"

"No, Katia. You will not move me on this. I do my duty to him, that is enough."

Fucking male pride.

"I heard that."

I rolled over and gave him my back. "Good. I'm glad."

Wasn't it enough that we were together now? Couldn't we just forgive and forget? Couldn't we just move on from the past and look to the future?

Damn it! I didn't want to harbor any more grudges, or have any more regrets. I wanted everything to work out! I wanted a perfect happy ending to this tale of grief and loss that is my life.

Am I asking for too much?

I guess so.

Stoyan put his hand on my shoulder. "Katia, look at me."

I shrugged him off. "I'm tired."

He rolled me over anyway. "I am sorry. I do not want to fight with you. You are right. The most important thing is that we are together. We should think of the future and let go of the past. If talking to my father again will make you happy, then that is what I will do."

Wow. That was easy.

Stoyan frowned. "I heard that."

I kissed him on the nose. "Thank you. I really just want to start over. By the way, how do you hear my thoughts so easily now?"

He smiled. "Your heart is very open at the moment," he whispered. He cupped my chin and placed a searing kiss on lips. "Wouldn't it be nice if we had a grandchild to bring back for my parents?"

The thought terrified me beyond words. I imagined a little girl with Stoyan's hair and my gifts, her life forever in danger from ghosts and demons and—

I wiggled out from under Stoyan. "No, no children."

"Katia, she would have a protector. It is something that comes with the gift. It will be predestined. Her protector will be the love of her life."

I jumped out of the bed and went to my dresser. "No, there are too few protectors left in the world."

Shit. I was stupid to think this would work out. Worse, we'd just had sex—without protection. I could already be pregnant.

Pulling out my pj's, I threw them on, never once glancing at Stoyan.

"Wait, Katia. We need to talk." Stoyan said, climbing out of bed and going to his suitcase.

I could hear Charlie whining at the back door. Grateful for an excuse, I rushed from the bedroom.

"Stop, Katia!" I heard Stoyan holler.

"I'm just letting Charlie in," I responded as I exited the hall.

I came to an abrupt halt.

Red.

My walls had the words *Find Angel* all over them, written in bright red.

"Katia!"

I glanced over my shoulder to see Stoyan bolt out of the bedroom and run toward me.

Charlie's ferocious barking filled my ears.

I swung back around and found myself staring into black eyes and a mouth full of sharp teeth.

CHAPTER ELEVEN

With one touch, I knew his whole life. Now I was to witness his death.

I watched the ten year-old little girl washing dishes. Angel was daydreaming of better days, dreaming of the times her brother spoke of, when he would be sixteen and they would run away from home. Then, Jacob could quit school and be able to get a job to support them both.

But Jacob had just turned fifteen. They still had a whole year to go.

The soapy glass slid out of her hand, bounced on the edge of the counter, hit the dirty floor and shattered. She held her breath, hoping the incident went unheard.

Fear filled her eyes as the stomping, booted feet entered the kitchen.

"Stupid, fucking kid," her drunken father roared, flinging little Angel into the kitchen table.

Jacob ran in. "I got it, dad. I'll clean it up," he said, collecting the broom and dustpan from the corner.

"Fucking kids! Useless. The both of you."

Angel whimpered. She was trying to remove the chunk of glass from her leg. It hurt and was bleeding everywhere.

This enraged the drunken father. He didn't like crying. It showed weakness. And he wasn't going to raise wussy kids.

Grabbing her by the hair, he dragged Angel across the glass-strewn floor. "Stop being a fucking baby," he raged. "It only hurts if you let it."

Jacob jumped on his arm. "Stop dad! She's wearing shorts, you're cutting her more."

The father pushed Jacob off, sending him careening into the counter.

"Then she won't wear shorts again, will she?" he bellowed above Angel's screaming, still sliding the child around.

Jacob was on his feet and back at his father, pounding at the large man with his fists. "Let her go!"

Angel was momentarily forgotten.

I closed my eyes, I couldn't watch.

The sounds were bad enough.

* * * *

"You can open your eyes," Jacob said quietly.

I did so slowly, expecting to see the worse. Thankfully, we were no longer at his house. Jacob looked normal again. No more fangs or ink black eyes.

We were on my back patio. Behind us was Charlie, standing on his hind legs with his paws on the door, his mouth opened in mid-bark. Charlie was moving so slowly, he might as well have been suspended in time.

Looking though the clear plastic that covered the small windows of the French doors, I saw my body trapped in a seemingly perpetual, but definitely gradual fall.

Shit.

When my body hit the floor, I would probably be dead.

It takes only a few seconds for the body to shut down when there is no life force present in it. Then I, my spirit self, standing on the patio now, would disappear, my soul lost forever.

If it wasn't for the kid's intense power that allowed him to speed up time on his plane of existence, I'd probably already be gone. It was weird to be ten seconds from death on one plane of existence, and ten minutes from death on another.

Stuck also in this near frozen world was Stoyan, his arm flung out as if to pull me back. I was just out of his reach, his fingers only inches away.

My dear Stoyan…I would never see him again.

I wanted to cry. I wanted to sit on that deck and bawl my eyes out…for Jacob and his loss…and for my own. I wanted to scream about the injustice of it all. I wanted to rage at the universe, at God, at everything.

But I didn't. It would have been a waste of what little time I had left.

"I can't find my sister. Can you help me?" Jacob asked.

I exhaled a heavy breath. "I can't."

"Why?"

I pointed to my body inside the kitchen. "You took my soul."

The kid looked down and wrinkled his brow.

"I'm dying. Once I do, I will disappear."

"To where?" he asked.

"Nowhere."

"You won't go to heaven?"

"Nope."

"Why?"

"There is no one around to lead me there," I replied.

"Why do you need someone to lead you?"

How could I explain such complicated matters to a child? And should I bother?

Fuck it, why not? It seemed I had nothing but time at the moment.

"When you are dying, your soul sends out a kind of cosmic call saying, 'come get me'. If you are meant to go to heaven, someone from there will come to collect you.

Usually, it's a dead relative or an angel. If you are going to hell, a demon will come. If you are going someplace else or being reincarnated, some other being will come collect you and lead you to where you need to be."

"No one came to get me. My mom died when Angel was born."

My life was like a broken record—his mother, my mother, my mother's mother. "I know. I saw that when you touched me. I'm sorry."

Though he tried to keep a brave face, I could see the worry in his eyes.

"Why didn't my mom come? Or an angel?"

"Sometimes the call is delayed because of a deed undone, or an issue unresolved. Once you've found your sister, your soul will send the call out and you'll move on."

His relief was evident.

"Why is it different for you?" he asked.

"Normally, you have to be dying for the call to go out. You took my soul before I was dying."

"Why won't the call sound later for you like it will for me?"

"There is no need for a call to go out. My soul has been collected."

"By who?"

"By you."

"I don't get it."

Yeah, I knew how he felt. I sat down on my patio chair, trying to remember the way my grandma explained it to me when I was young.

"Usually, a soul is attached to a body. The soul cannot leave the body unless the body is dying. When the body is dying, the soul sends out a call. This call is not like an intercom call going out everywhere to everyone; it is more like a telephone call. This cosmic call goes to one the specific being in charge of collecting your soul."

I stopped my explanation and made a sign toward the other chair. Jacob sat down in it.

Rules of Darkness

"When the call is received, that specific being comes and leads the soul away. This all happens in the matter of seconds. By the time the body is actually dead, the soul is already where it needs to be. Are you still with me?"

The kid nodded.

"I'm different because my soul is free. My soul can leave my body without me being in the throes of death. Because you are a spirit, you are technically a soul collector. You touched me and collected my soul. But since I wasn't dying when you touched me my soul never sent out the call to the being that would have normally collected it. So you still have possession of my soul. Do you follow?"

He nodded again.

I don't think Jacob really understood what I was saying. I mean, I had just told a fifteen year-old kid that he had possession of my soul, and he nodded like it was no big deal.

I pressed on, "Now, the difference between you and me is this: You fall under a cosmic loop hole. You were dying, but your soul did not send out a call, so it was not collected. So it went into the spirit world. However, your soul is still unbound—not collected. When it finds peace, it will send out a call and you will be collected and led to wherever. However, I was not dying. My soul did not send out a call. But my soul was still collected—by you. Soul collectors only have limited time to lead the soul to where it needs to be and drop it off."

"How much time is that?" Jacob asked

"The amount of time between dying and actual death…or the amount of time between soul collection and the body's death. Even if the body is healthy, without the soul in it, the body dies. The soul can live without a body, but a body cannot live without a soul."

"So what's going to happen to you?"

Just as I witnessed your death, you will witness mine. "As my body dies, my soul will be lost and fade away into nothing."

"Why?"

"Because you have collected my soul, led me through your life, and then dropped me here on my back porch. But my back porch is not a place that holds souls. Heaven, hell, living bodies, these are soul receptacles. If my body dies, and you have not brought me to the place that holds souls, then my soul will be taken away from you. The universe will absorb my soul into itself and I will cease to exist."

I saw the realization dawn in his eyes.

Jacob shot up from the chair. "I didn't know you would die if I touched you. I only wanted your help. You were the only person that could see me and I just want to find my sister and you wouldn't help me. So I found a way in—"

"I know, Jacob. It's okay. I don't blame you for anything."

He paced the patio, still clearly agitated by the situation he had inadvertently put me in.

I suddenly felt horrible. It wasn't my intention to make him feel guilty.

Having been a witness to his life, I knew Jacob really wasn't a bad kid. When he was alive, his peers were wary of him. He was quick to anger, picked fights, seemed fearless. But what no one realized was that he actually had a soft heart, one that made him want to protect those weaker than him, like his sister. No one ever noticed that he only picked fights with bullies, usually to stop them from tormenting some other poor kid.

Jacob never preyed on those weaker than him. He didn't believe in that. That was what his father did. And he didn't want to be like his father.

He loved animals, and he loved his mother very much. He kept a picture of her hidden in his room. When he was alone, he would pull it out and talk to her.

Rules of Darkness   105

I shrugged and forced a smile. "Look, Jacob. It's fine. I'll be okay, really. Being absorbed into the universe is not necessarily a bad thing. If anything, I'm kind of excited about embarking on a new adventure."

Okay, it was a cheesy lie. And the skeptical look he gave me said he knew I was full of shit.

The kid went back to the patio door and gazed longingly inside. "I'm really sorry. I wasn't trying to hurt you. Even when I did all those things with your car and the dog, it was an accident. It was weird, I would think something and it would happen, even if I didn't mean for it to, but was just thinking it because I was mad that you wouldn't help me. And then that guy kept sending me away."

"Stoyan. My husband."

"He can see me?"

"Um…I don't think so. Not the way I can. I think he sees your presence. I think he sees you like a blob of light, or a white shapeless cloud or something. I'm not sure."

Funny. Stoyan never did discuss the situation about the kid with me. I guess with everything else going on, we just never got around to talking about it.

Jacob turned back, his eyes wide. "Hey! Can I lead you to heaven?"

Poor kid, he sounded so hopeful.

I pretended to consider the possibility. I shrugged. "Do you know how to get there?"

His face fell. "No."

"It's okay. But thanks for thinking of me."

His face brightened again. "You said that your soul could go into a living body? Your body is still alive, right? Can I take you back to your body?"

It was a feasible idea, but…

"We can't get into the house. The doors are locked."

Jacob actually beamed with pride. "I can walk through doors now. That's how I got in earlier."

I had to smile. Yes, even on the verge of death and nonexistence, I was actually having a good time talking to the kid.

"And do you remember how hard that was? How much power and concentration it took for you to go through the door?"

He nodded.

"Now imagine double the effort. You would have to drag me with you."

"Why can't you go through the door yourself?" he asked.

"I have no power in this state. I'm attached to you, sharing your plane of existence."

"Why are the doors so hard to go through?"

"By nature, locked doors have magical properties. Spirits usually can't pass through them, hence the reason they feel compelled to knock. Once in a while, a spirit will have enough power to pass through a locked door, but that's very rare."

"Why can't we go through windows? Or break down walls and go in that way?"

"Because that is not what windows and walls are made for. Spirits have to follow different rules than they did in life. If the spirit has the power to do so, it may destroy anything it is inclined to, like you did with my SUV. But spirits still cannot enter a place unless through a door."

Jacob got all exited. "I think I can break down the door. I almost did the last times I tried. I should have enough power to do that."

He turned, picked up Charlie and propped him against the patio railing. Returning to the door, he stood in front of it, focusing hard.

I leaned back in my chair and watched, trying not to get my hopes up, telling myself that it didn't matter one way or another if the kid was successful.

Three unseen knocks echoed off the door.

The blows against the wood sounded normal here, nothing like the resonant booming that emerged in the physical world.

Thump, thump, thump.

Strange the way things are perceived when experiencing it from another plane of existence. It was as if sight and sound became distorted when it crossed over dimensional boundaries.

"Jacob, when we first met, I spoke to you. Could you hear me?"

Thump, thump, thump.

"It was muffled, like I had earplugs in. You said you couldn't help me."

"Just wondering. You know, I can't hear you."

Thump, thump, thump.

"I figured that out. Sorry I wrote all over your walls. I didn't know how else to ask for your help."

"No problem. It's only paint, right?" Please let it have been red paint.

"Yeah. If I get you back to your body, will you try to help me find my sister?"

"Of course."

"Promise?"

"Promise."

My answer must have excited him. The knocking became faster in succession.

...thump, thump, thump...

..thump, thump, thump...

My heart leapt with joy when the door started giving way under Jacob's incessant beating. This plan might actually work.

...thump, thump, thump...

...thump, thump, thump...

The door's hinges were loosening.

Suddenly, a strange sensation filled me. I looked down, only to see that my legs had turned translucent. I could see the chair beneath my lap.

Fuck! I was starting to fade. We were running out of time.

"Jacob! Hurry!"

He looked over his shoulder, his eyes going wide with fear. "I'm trying! Don't go yet! I'm almost through!"

…thump, thump, thump…

…thump, thump, thump…

Don't go yet? What did the kid want me to do? I couldn't stop something like this.

…thump, thump, thump…

There was a flash of light.

Stoyan stood beside me.

He grabbed my arm.

Chapter Twelve

I was yanked up before I hit the floor.

A loud crack reverberated through the roaring wind and whirling debris.

Stoyan pulled me against his chest and covered my head with his hand. He chanted foreign words in rhythmic commands

There was an explosion near where we stood.

A burst of energy shot from Stoyan, encompassing the room in a flash of white light.

The wind suddenly died, followed by the shattering of windborne objects crashing to the floor. An eerie silence descended around us.

What the hell had just happened?

Insistent barking filled the air.

I pulled out of Stoyan's embrace and raised my head. My patio doors were obliterated.

I scanned the room. "Where's the kid?"

"I banished him," Stoyan replied.

"Shit!" I tried to run to the patio, but Stoyan captured my hand.

"No, Katia. The glass… you have no shoes on."

Fuck. Destruction was everywhere. And poor Charlie was barking his head off before the doorway, desperately wanting to enter the house, but waiting for permission.

I ran into the bedroom. Lifting the blinds, I searched the back yard, hoping to see Jacob lingering outside the barrier somewhere.

Nothing. Jacob was gone.

I smacked my palm against the window.

I heard Stoyan come into the room.

"Where did you send him?" I asked.

"The farthest I could. Since his existence mirrors our own, he should be half a world away."

China? He sent the poor kid to China?

"Bring him back," I demanded.

"No."

I spun around. "Damn it! Why? Why did you do that? Why did you banish him? I promised I'd help him."

"He is dangerous," Stoyan replied evenly.

"Dangerous?" I threw up my arms. "He's just a kid. I can't believe you sent him off to fucking Asia."

"Katia, I will not apologize for what I did. My first priority is your safety. Jacob might be a child, but he is also a powerful spirit; that makes him dangerous. It might not be his intention to cause harm, but the risk is there all the same."

"Yeah, whatever," I muttered as I pushed past him to leave.

I didn't make it out the door.

His fingers closed around my arm and swung me around. "You almost lost your soul tonight! Wake up, Katia. This is not a fucking game."

Can we say stunned stupid? That was me. My dropped jaw refused to form words. Not only did he yell at me, he swore! He actually used a curse word!

Releasing his hold, Stoyan stepped back and looked away. He balled his hand and tapped it against his lips, as if willing himself to remain silent until he calmed down.

Finally, his gaze locked on mine. Besides his anger, I saw something in the depths of his eyes that I had never seen there before.

Fear? Desperation? Indecision?

In Stoyan?

Why?

Instantly, I found the answer to "why" reflected in those depths.

I might as well have been standing in front of a mirror.

It was because of me. He was afraid of what I would do, of what choices I'd make, and unsure of how to protect me when I insisted on putting myself in danger.

And he was terrified of failing me.

God, I was doing it again, wasn't I? I was letting my heart rule me. I was making rash decisions without thinking about the consequences those actions might have on my life and those around me.

Worse than that, I was not letting Stoyan in, not trusting him to come through for me, though minutes earlier, he had saved my life.

Tears blurred my vision. He was so worried about failing me, but he never had. If anything, I was the one always failing him.

"I'm sorry. I told myself I would stop being so impulsive, but I guess bad habits are tough to break. I'll try harder to change."

Shaking his head, he gathered me in his arms. "Katia, I do not want you to change. I love you as you are. I always have. I just want you to be safe. I want to have a life with you…" He let out a heavy breath, and pulled me tight against him. "A very *long,* happy life," he said against my ear.

"You didn't fail me. You saved me. You gathered my soul before it was lost."

"You were only gone a few seconds, but it felt like an eternity. I do not know what I would have done if I had lost you."

If he only knew how long a few seconds really was.

"Thank you for saving me. I should have said that earlier."

"You, my love, never need to thank me." Stoyan nudged my head back, wiped my tears with his thumbs, and then kissed my cheeks. "We will help Jacob find his sister, but we will do it safely—"

"Wait a minute. How do you know his name? How do you know he's looking for his sister?"

"When I left you earlier, I went to town to do research on recent deaths in the hopes of finding out the identity of the spirit."

"How did you know you had the right one?"

"This area is just a gathering of small towns. Not many violent deaths concerning minors occur around here."

"Okay, so how did you figure out that it was a minor haunting me and not some adult? You never asked me."

Stoyan chuckled. "Because you kept referring to the spirit as 'that kid'."

"Stoyan. Do you know where his sister is?"

"I do."

* * * *

Under the guise of a 'concerned teacher' visiting her student, I stood over the small hospital bed and looked down upon the innocent girl, noting how much her name fit her in this moment. The bruises on her face were now faded, her soft hair was brushed to the side, no doubt by a caring nurse, and her eyes hidden behind tender lids.

She was a beautiful child. Truly angelic in her rest, her expression was one of peace.

However, I knew the truth. She was far from peaceful.

I could hear the screams echoing in her head.

She was lost in a nightmarish place, her mind trapped in a perpetual loop that replayed the same terrible scenes over and over again.

I knew where she was imprisoned. I heard the moments she repeatedly endured. Horrid sounds formed the images in my mind, burned them to my soul, and left a mark upon me that I would carry the rest of my life.

I took a breath to ease my nauseous stomach. Since I had insisted on ignoring my gift for so long, I wasn't used to the intrusion of another's experiences.

It had been twelve years since I'd opened my mind to another. Twelve years since I'd laid hands upon a lost one and wished it peace. I was not certain I could do this. What if I failed?

"Where's the father?" I asked.

"Committed suicide," Stoyan replied quietly.

"Does she have family?"

"No."

My hands trembled as I raised them from my side and settled on Angel's temples. I pulled back. I wanted to heal her, but...

"She didn't come to me, you know. The lost ones have to come to me. I'm not supposed to seek them out. It's one of the rules. Fate chooses the one to receive healing; I'm not supposed to play God."

"She did come to you."

"No, her brother did."

Stoyan raised my hand and placed it on my chest, covering it with his own. "What does your heart say?"

"It says I should heal her. But, Stoyan, of course my heart would want that. My heart rules me."

He removed my hand and brought it to his lips. "And I love that about you, Katia."

His reassurance gave me strength.

I would heal her, and I would accept the consequences, be they good or bad.

I placed my fingers back on Angel's temples, asking God to grant her peace.

Her mind quieted. Her eyes fluttered open.

For a few moments, she stared at us, dazed, confused. Suddenly, her eyes closed. The screams filled her mind again.

I shook my head. "Something is wrong."

"Try again," Stoyan whispered.

I did, but it happened again. She came out and went back in.

Oh, please don't let this happen. Lord, don't trap this poor little girl in that mental hell.

Tears welled in my eyes as I tried a third time. Unsuccessful.

It was too much for me. I broke.

"I can't heal her," I sobbed. "Her mind, her memory, it dominates her world."

Stoyan leaned over, placing his hand on Angel's.

"Do it again, Katia."

"I can't do it. It won't work. I can only heal the pain. Heal the sickness. I can't erase memories."

"Do you trust me?" he asked softly.

Nodding, I tried again. But this time, when Angel's eyes opened, Stoyan began chanting. When he finished, her dazed look cleared.

I laughed with joy that knew no boundaries. "We did it! What did you...?"

Stoyan's eyes were closed, but a tear escaped and rolled down his cheek.

The healing worked, but at what cost?

"You have your father's gift? You carry the memory?"

Before Stoyan could respond, Angel let out a gasp. "What's wrong with Jacob?"

I followed her gaze.

Jacob stood in the doorway.

I guess now that Angel was free of the prison in her mind, her brother was able to locate her. Jacob had lost the two-inch razor teeth and horrific mask of rage, but still had his big black eyes and sad gaping mouth.

I wondered how I could explain to Angel that she was seeing her brother's ghost...but then, I wondered how she was able to see him at all. When I saw her life through the eyes of her brother, she held no such gift.

Jacob suddenly disappeared.

Rules of Darkness

Angel's eyes went bright. "Mommy?" She then frowned "Why is Jacob going with you?"

I looked at Stoyan. "Why can't I see him?" I mouthed.

He leaned over and whispered in my ear, "You can only see the unsettled. Jacob's mother has come for him. He has found peace now."

"How can she see them?" I whispered back.

"This is a common, temporary gift of sight for the one left behind. It is so they might find closure by having the opportunity to say goodbye."

Angel pulled back the covers. "I want to go too."

Sitting up, the young girl moved her legs to the edge of the mattress to get out of the bed. Suddenly, she stopped.

"Okay, mommy, I'll listen."

After a few moments of silence, Angel started to cry, nodding the way children do when a parent is telling them something important.

Angel looked at us, and then turned back to the doorway. "But I don't want a new mommy and daddy. Why can't you and Jacob stay here?"

Stoyan slid his arms around my shoulders and pulled me close as I wept.

The little girl wiped her cheeks. "Okay, I promise."

I clutched tightly to Stoyan's shirt. "Can you hear them?"

He shook his head. "No, I can only see their light and it is fading now. They are leaving."

"I—I love you too," Angel hiccupped, then fell back into her bed, and bawled into her pillow.

Epilogue

Eighteen months later…

I had been here a week, and I still couldn't believe this place was once my home. At sixteen, I left here in tears, imbedding in my mind a memory of resentment, and impracticality. I'd even wished a hole would open in the earth and swallow the archaic village.

How wrong I was.

Today, the village was a place of hope, understanding, and love for mankind. It was a retreat for those searching for their inner gifts, an environment to hone the ones they were aware of, and above all, it was a sanctuary for those in need of healing.

I was amazed at how much Stoyan had accomplished in twelve short years. It was a massive project given to him when he first obtained his Master's Degree in international business and started working for his father.

The outskirts of the village were no longer barren fields that refused to yield food. Now a hotel with a pool, spa, restaurants, and conference rooms occupied the land.

Inside the village, where there had once been only shacks of wood and stone, there were now small cottages complete with electricity and running water. Home again to the people who, like myself, had once fled this place wanting to integrate into the normal world. Many had come back here to live and work, and contribute to the continuance of our heritage and our gifts.

In the center of the village was a large grassy square where people communed to give or receive guidance and healing, to simply sit and talk, to learn, or to do things as mundane as shop for trinkets at one of the many stalls. It was the perfect place to read a book, paint a picture, or have a cup of coffee with a friend.

A soft breeze swept over me as I walked through the crowded square. Though barely audible, I could hear the whispers of the departed elders preaching for the young ones. *Remember your gifts and use them wisely. Be an honorable force in the world.*

If they were here now, I think the elders would have been pleased with the evolution of our village, despite the modern upgrades. I believe they would have been happy to see our slice of the earth pulsate with life again and be filled with the laughter of children, the love of family, and the pride of heritage.

I rested my hand over my bulging tummy.

Would my children grow to know this place? Would they love it? I didn't know for sure if the baby was a boy or a girl, but I had a feeling I would be blessed with a daughter.

Would she come back to this place in the summers to learn our customs and explore her gifts with the elders that resided here?

Anxiety nearly overwhelmed me.

My eyes instantly sought and located Stoyan a short distance away, engaged in a conversation with his father. He turned and met my gaze, giving me a reassuring smile, as if he knew my thoughts—which he probably did.

If it was another daughter, and she happened to inherit my gifts, she would be well cared for. Fate would find a way to bring her a protector.

"Are you okay, honey?" I asked, looking over my shoulder.

"I'm okay," Angel replied, seeming lost in her own world as she wandered around a small booth behind me, filled with crystals and other such things.

For a little girl who'd just turned twelve, Angel was too reserved, too old in her ways.

I peered out over the grass where the other kids had gathered to listen to an elder reciting a story. Angel should want to be over there, laughing, having fun, *wanting* to hang out with other boys and girls her age.

But she didn't.

She still grieved for her brother.

Even though Stoyan took from her the gruesome images of how Jacob died, Angel bore many memories from her tragic life. Her brother had been her strength for the first decade of her existence, and now he was gone. It was a void that no amount of love and caring could fill.

My heart ached for her.

Stoyan and his parents approached us, bringing along an older couple. During the introductions, I was told by the man and his wife that they knew of me, for I was legend to our people.

What?

They threw words out like *powerful healer of the lost*, and then spoke of my great-grandmother.

It turned out they were relatives of one of the families I'd stayed with during my travels.

The older man then referred to the kids surrounding the tale-telling elder, pointing out twin boys who sat on the grass in the very back of the group...with the group, but somehow still apart.

"My grandsons," he said, his voice filled with pride, "both hold the gifts of the protector."

Delight fluttered on the breeze, a tinkling sound, as familiar as it was foreign. Realizing Angel was no longer with us, I scanned the area.

Rules of Darkness

Angel sat on a blanket with an old woman. The wise elder with long black hair and exotic eyes leaned over and placed something around Angel's neck. For a fleeting moment, a gold glow descended upon them.

I panicked.

"Stoyan!" I gasped, before hurrying over to Angel.

I fell to my knees beside my daughter, sparing an accusing glare at the elder.

"What have you done?" I demanded.

The elder smiled and said something in a language I did not understand.

Angel beamed. "She says she's given to me what is already mine. She has been waiting for me to come for a long time."

I gently lifted the thin chain around my daughter's neck and studied the gold amulet: An image of the Egyptian goddess, Bastet.

"Angel, how do you understand Arabic now?"

She shrugged. "I don't. My special friend told me what she said."

Stoyan, Stylianos and Ileana quickly joined us. "What's happening," my mother-in-law asked in concern.

Glancing away for a moment, Angel nodded, as if engaged in some conversation with an imaginary playmate.

My daughter turned to me. "My guide wants me to tell you that Jackie sends her regards," Angel relayed with curious innocence. She then wrinkled her nose. "Who's Jackie? What's a regard?"

"Stoyan, what do we do?" I whispered, horrified.

He knelt beside me, "If it was not destined, it would not have happened."

That brought me little comfort.

Stoyan glanced at our daughter, and then at the elder. "Are you to be her mentor?" he asked in our people's tongue.

The elder nodded, her eyes showing how pleased she was with this.

"Oh, I forgot!" Angel exclaimed.

"What?" I asked cautiously, almost afraid to learn the answer.

"When my new friend came, she brought messages from my brother." Excitement sparkled in her eyes. "One message was for you! My brother told my guide to tell me to tell you thanks!"

I couldn't find my voice to respond.

Angel was glowing, her happiness radiating like the sun. My daughter was not the same girl she had been when she woke up that morning.

Angel started to laugh. Pointing to the group of children, she said, "My guide said my sister will one day marry—"

Palms covered my ears.

A muted exchange occurred.

Stoyan lifted his hands just as Angel giggled her promise 'to keep the surprise a secret'.

My hand flew to my mouth as I tried to hold in the overwhelming emotions. I failed miserably.

I fell into Stoyan's arms, sobbing.

My husband held me close as I cried tears of joy and relief into his chest. I didn't have to worry for my unborn daughter anymore. Somewhere in that group of children, her future protector waited.

After placing a kiss atop of my head, he murmured in my ear. "I love you, Katia."

I looked up into his knowing eyes.

He read my heart.

Read on for a preview of Tia Fanning's
Rules of Fire, book two in the Rules series.

Coming in 2008 to
www.resplendencepublishing.com
and
www.amazon.com

CHAPTER ONE

They say that in the final moments before your death, your whole life flashes before your eyes.

That is not always true.

Yes, the crowded room around me has become nothing more than smears of brilliant color, unrecognizable and grotesque. And I no longer smell the sickly scent of sweat and perfume mingling with the pungent aroma of alcohol and marijuana. Nor do I feel the biting pain of countless fingers pressing into my body as they drag me toward my doom, despite my desperate struggle to halt the advance. My pleading screams, lost and ignored in the deafening revelry, have faded into dull murmurs, replaced with the rapid thumping of my terrified heart.

In this moment I should see it all—my whole life racing across my vision like a movie on sonic fast-forward. But I do not see images from my tragic childhood, nor do I see the faces of my family.

I only replay one day from my life

The day I turned fourteen.

* * * *

"Angel, this is a special day for you," my mentor remarked in my parents' native language. "In the times long past, the first birthday that came after the start of a girl's menses was celebrated as her entrance into womanhood."

I nodded, feeling my cheeks grow warmer, despite the fact that I was already hot and sticky. Wasn't it bad enough that I was riding a smelly camel through a barren desert in search of some hidden temple? Did my mentor really need to talk about my period in front of my grandfather?

"I think you are embarrassing her, Elder Mahin," my grandpa remarked casually.

Damn. Did he always know everything?

"Nonsense," she replied. "It is the natural order of things, like the phases of the moon. Why would your granddaughter be embarrassed over her monthly cycle? You are her grandfather, are you not?"

My cheeks went from warm to scalding. *Oh God, kill me now.*

I heard my guide giggle in my head.

Shaking my head, I let out a heavy breath. *Why did we have to bring grandpa again?*

Because in these days, two women venturing out into the desert alone would have attracted attention. He is our escort.

I adjusted my head dress for the millionth time. The damn thing didn't want to stay up. *How much longer to the temple? I'm friggin sweating my ass off out here!*

Language, language… It is not far.

Ignoring the subtle reprimand, I pressed on. *Did you take Elder Mahin here when she was fourteen?*

No, she was sixteen. She started her menses later than you.

My guide slipped away from my mind. I searched around, finding my friend's golden radiance floating on the wind, keeping pace a few yards ahead of the camels. She usually resided as a voice in my head, her presence no louder than a thought, but once in a while, when it suited her, she'd take form apart from me.

It was pretty cool to have a guide. She was like my

best friend. After losing my brother, Jacob, I thought my life unbearable. Even though my adopted parents were wonderful to me, I just couldn't seem to find happiness in anything. But then I met Elder Mahin.

Elder Mahin once said she had been worried because she was getting old, and the guide had not chosen her next companion yet, but then fate brought me into their lives. Her guide passed to me, and Elder Mahin became my mentor. As my mentor, she teaches me how to use my gifts to help the world.

There it is.

I looked ahead to where my guide hovered, but saw nothing.

The temple is hidden by magic, but it will come into view for those who truly want to find it.

I guess it was pretty obvious that I didn't care if I found the temple or not. Unless...

Does it have air conditioning?

No. But it has shade.

That was good enough for me.

Squinting in the distance, through the waves of heat rising from the sand, I spied the beginnings of a surface glinting in the sunlight. Beyond the rippled glare, a large structure emerged, half buried in the dunes.

As we drew closer, we passed by the enormous monument guarding the entrance of the temple, reminding me very much of the sphinx that stood before the pyramids in Giza. However, this huge statue depicted the sphinx from the Greek legends, with the face and breasts of a woman, the body of a lioness, and the wings of an eagle, neatly folded back upon its feline back.

I turned and looked over my shoulder, almost expecting the large stone eyes to open wide and the mouth to come alive, demanding that we answer a riddle.

"You ladies go ahead. I will await you here," my grandfather said as we dismounted.

The shimmering essence that was my guide went on

toward the entrance. Elder Mahin followed, signaling for me to keep up. We passed under a large-shouldered, flat arch into what seemed to be a long tunnel lit by hundreds of candles that sat upon the walls.

"Is there anyone here?" I whispered as we headed deeper into the cool darkness.

"No," my mentor replied. "Magic keeps this place."

I silently followed, then saw the shadows cast upon the walls. Two people following... a cat? I looked ahead and saw only my guide. The further we went in, the brighter my guide glowed, and the larger the shadowed cat on the wall grew, becoming more and more like a tigress or lioness.

By the time the entrance was out of view, and the soft glow of the candles was the only light available, the hallway opened into a large columned room. In the center stood a huge golden shrine of the goddess Bastet surrounded by flowers, burning incense, and perfume bottles. Along the inner walls of the temple were paintings of women, sphinxes, and other feline creatures.

In awe, I turned to my guide, only to find that her feline shadow had spouted wings, replicating the large monument that guarded the front of the temple.

"You're a sphinx?" I gasped.

I heard my guide's voice, not inside my head, but as a light whisper floating on the scented smoke. "Yes. That is one of many names for my kind."

Suddenly, my guide took off, frolicking around the statue of Basset with the excitement of a kitten pouncing on a ball of yarn.

I looked to my mentor. "I thought she was good? In Greek mythology, didn't the sphinx like...eat people? Just because they couldn't answer a stupid riddle?"

Elder Mahin clucked her tongue. "She *is* good. You cannot always rely on legends of man to judge a creature. Like most beings of this world, her kind has been granted free will, and can choose whether to be a good force or an evil force. In most cultures, sphinxes are revered as protectors who ward off evil."

"Why is she a guide then?"

"As human civilization came to dominate the world, man became fearful of any creature that possessed intelligence and magic, and hunted those creatures to near extinction. God took pity on those being hunted and gave them the ability to flee this world."

"So the creatures that star in bedtime stories—dragons, unicorns, fairies and all that—were once real?" I asked skeptically.

"They are real now. Some still reside in our world as they were, and some reside here in a different form, as your guide does. Others fled into different realms, and some move in between planes of existence. It all depends."

I glanced around the temple. "Why are we here again?"

"So you may come to know your gift better. So you can pay homage to the Goddess that gave you your gift."

"Um, isn't that blasphemy against God? I mean, Bastet is one of the gods from Egyptian mythology."

"God is God, no matter the form. Male, female, one or many." Moving over to a candle, my mentor placed her fingers near the flame, so close that the glow radiated off her skin. "It's like comparing *light* to *rays of light*. Are they not one in the same? You can see the light from this candle illuminate my hand. Is it one light? Or is it many rays of light that shine on me?

I shrugged. "I think it's many. I learned in school that light has different wavelengths. Light can be split up with a prism."

"Ah, yes, this is true. But what is color but the perception of light? Perhaps some think of light as the white glow, but others may acknowledge light by the many colors that appear once the darkness has been chased away. God is like this. Some see God as one encompassing all, like the brightness that shines from the sun, and some choose to acknowledge God like they would a rainbow, seeing instead the many different hues. Answer me this: Which is the correct way to perceive light? By the white light that goes into a prism? Or the many colors that come out?"

I shook my head. "That question doesn't make any sense. There is no right way or wrong way to see it. It's all the same."

"Exactly."

Okay, she had kind of lost me, but I smiled like I understood *exactly* what she meant, even if I wasn't quite getting her whole philosophy-theology speech.

After a moment of tense silence, I shrugged. "Am I allowed to look around?" Upon Elder Mahin's nod, I ventured away to explore the chamber.

I started near the entrance, and then slowly walked the chamber's wall, studying the many life-size paintings and symbols that covered the stone. Obviously, this place had been around a while. I had no idea what the symbols represented, but the perfectly preserved art work depicted how the world was perceived thousands of years ago through the eyes of those who practiced magic, walked with 'gods', and lived in myth. The artwork didn't reflect any one style. It was more like a blend of many: Greek, Roman, Egyptian, Mesopotamian, Indian, Persian, Chinese, and some I didn't recognize. It was as if artists from all the great ancient civilizations journeyed to this temple for an international painting party.

As I neared the rear wall, a painted scene drew my attention, seeming to come to life amid the flickering candle light and dancing shadows. Rubbing my hand along the wall, I started to fabricate a story...

"Once upon a time," I whispered, "there was a beautiful girl who was traveling through the desert looking for her lost camel. She really didn't want to find the smelly animal, but her grandfather insisted that she retrieve the stinky creature. During her search under the blistering desert sun, she saw a ring lying on the sand. As the girl didn't have a mom who had to follow a set of weird rules, she had never heard the warning that one shouldn't pick up random objects that lie upon the ground. So, her dumb ass not only picked up the ring, but put it on."

My fingers trailed over to the back wall. I saw a small salamander and snatched my hand back before I ran over it.

"How did you get here? There is no water near by, is there?"

I gathered the little red and charcoal-colored critter in my hand. The salamander sat on my palm, seeming not to fear me. I raised it higher to get a better look.

Maybe there was some underwater spring or something.

Shrugging, I returned my free hand to the painted scene, and turned my other hand so the salamander could see the paintings too. "This is where the monster appears," I explained to my new friend. "The monster kidnaps the girl and drags her off to his castle in hell. Thankfully, the ugly monster was fascinated with the girl's beauty, so he didn't kill her. But he did unspeakable things to her body."

Giving an exaggerated sigh, I shook my head in feigned pity and moved further down the wall. "The girl managed to escape. But the monster was angry, so he sent a giant bird to find the girl and kill her, which the bird did. However, as the bird looked upon the beauty of the dead girl, it became riddled with guilt. So, the bird flew the girl's lifeless body to the temple. The temple priestesses prepared the body and placed the girl on a funeral pyre. Overcome with shame, the giant bird committed suicide by flying into the raging fire consuming the dead girl's body. The end."

Giggling at my own stupidity, I lifted the salamander up to my face. "Wasn't that a good story?"

"That is not how it happened," the salamander quietly replied.

Dropping the amphibian, I jumped back and threw my hand over my mouth to keep from screaming.

I stared at the ground in horror. *Did I really just hear it talk?*

"Do not be afraid. I won't hurt you," the salamander assured me.

My palm smothered my squeal. *I did! I did hear it talk!*

"Angel?" my mentor called out from the opposite end of the chamber. "Are you doing well?"

Unable to find the strength to pull my hand away and unseal my lips, I shook my head 'no', though I knew Elder Mahin could not see my distress through the columned forest that stood between us.

"Please do not tell them about me. They will kill me," the salamander whispered.

In all honestly, I wanted to kill the demonic creature too. It had to be possessed!

My name echoed through the temple again.

"Please," he pleaded, fear tingeing his voice. "I only want to talk to you. I have not talked to anyone in such a long time. I am lonely. I will not hurt you. How can I hurt you? I am small."

The salamander seemed so scared, my terrified heart filled with pity. I slowly removed my hand. "Why—why would they want to kill you?"

He turned toward the mural on the wall. "I want tell you the true story. Do you want to hear what really happened?"

"Angel, where are you? Answer me," my mentor demanded.

I looked over my shoulder, then back at the salamander. "You didn't say why they would want to kill you."

"I have no time to tell you that story," he replied. "It is more important for you to know the true tale about the painting. But before I tell you, I want to show you the ring that started it all. May I show you the ring from the story? It will only take a moment."

"Angel!" My mentor called out again.

"Hold on. I'll be there in a sec," I hollered back.

I felt this overwhelming urge to see the ring in question, despite the scenes on the walls that clearly depicted a monster was attached to the band.

"If you want to see the ring, we must go now," he hissed.

I looked to the ground. "I'll only be gone a moment?"

The salamander raced up my leg, up my arm, and perched itself on my shoulder. "Touch the painting in front of you."

I placed my hand on the image of the funeral pyre. To my utter shock, instead of feeling cold stone beneath my fingers, my hand went through the rock and disappeared.

Gasping, I pulled my hand back out. "How? The wall was not like this before?"

"No time to explain. Let us go before the others come. You will like the ring. It is beautiful. And I will tell you the story. You will like it much more than the one shown here."

I knew I shouldn't go, that this might actually be the dumbest thing I'd ever done, but I closed my eyes and stepped into the wall, all the while wondering why I felt the overwhelming need to become the stupid girl in the horror movie that gets eaten by the monster.

I forced my feet to move. One step. Two steps. Three.

Taking a deep breath, I prepared myself for the worst. *Please don't let there be a monster.* I slowly open my eyes.

Fire.

It was the first thing I saw. In the middle of the chamber, there was a giant hearth that held a roaring fire. And the fire was massive, its flames reaching all the way to the ceiling. But surprisingly, the room wasn't hot, or even smoky. The flames didn't even scorch the ceiling black.

Glancing around, I noticed there was nothing else in the room. "Um, where is the ring?"

"It is floating in the flames."

Rules of Fire 131

I got as close to the fire as I dared, but still didn't see the ring.

"Closer," my shoulder companion urged.

"Yeah, you're out of your mind."

And I was out of my mind for listening to a talking amphibian in the first place. I turned to leave.

"Wait. I will tell you the story first."

With an exaggerated sigh, I stopped. "Hurry then."

"The woman in the story was a priestess of this temple. After visiting her family, she was journeying back here when she came upon the ring in the sand. When she put the ring on, a handsome prince appeared."

"Yeah, it looked more like a monster on the wall than a handsome prince," I remarked caustically, approaching one of the symbol-covered walls. The painted glyphs seemed ominous, the designs sharp, like it had been scribbled upon the stone with a sword.

"I tell you the truth. The mural you saw does not. It was a handsome prince from the land of fire Djinn. The prince fell in love with the girl and swept her away to his kingdom—"

"Don't you mean kidnapped?" I turned toward the hearth, searching again for the mysterious ring.

"No, no. She wanted to go with him. They were in love. They knew it the moment they saw each other," the salamander whispered. "It was love at first sight."

Mesmerized, I stared into the fire. I never realized how beautiful it all really was.

"They lived happily until one day, the priestesses put a secret spell out, summoning the woman back to the temple. The spell was so powerful, but so veiled, the prince didn't sense the presence of the magic. But the woman did. She tried to resist the spell, but she could not. As her feet forced her to leave her love behind, she came across a viper in the sand. She captured it and let it bite her, believing death would be better than living with a broken heart."

"That is so sad," I replied, walking closer to the

flames.

"As the woman lay dying in the sand, the prince felt her life force fading away, and knew his love was near death. He sent his most powerful ally, a phoenix, to find her, heal her, and bring her back to him."

I could see the ring. It was right there, so close.

"But the phoenix did not make it to her in time, and she died. Ashamed at his failure, the phoenix brought the woman here, back to the temple. As the priestesses put the woman's body on the funeral pyre, the prince appeared.

I lifted my arm and reached forward. The flames did not burn me.

"He placed a powerful spell upon the fire. He declared this fire would burn until the day his reincarnated love returned here, removed the ring from the flames, and placed it on her finger. Only she would be able to withstand the flames and claim what was hers."

My fingers clasped around the ring and pulled it out.

"Do you understand Angel? The ring was a token of their love, a love more powerful than death itself. And as the woman was wearing it when she died, she was still bound to the prince. It would not matter how many times his love lived and died, every lifetime, she would be compelled to spurn the afterlife and come back to this world."

I stared at the beautiful ring in my palm.

"The priestesses found the woman's first reincarnated soul in a baby born not too far from here. Knowing that the baby girl was capable of receiving a guide, and thus returning to the temple one day, they defied the girl's fate and sent the child far away to another land, to a place where magic was not known. The priestesses, who are able to communicate with spirits, contacted the child's soul collector and bid the spirit to never return the soul to a body where it could realize her destiny."

Is this ring mine?

"The priestesses thought they had overcome the spell,

Rules of Fire

as for many years and many lives, the woman lived and died, but never returned to claim the ring. Time passed, the world of magic faded, religion evolved and the old ways were lost, and some things were forgotten. Soon, the soul collector was the only one left who remembered."

The salamander scuttled down my arm onto my open palm.

He gazed up at me. "Though the soul collector chose the body of woman who knew nothing of this world, and deposited the soul in her womb, fate could no longer stand by and watch true love go unfulfilled. Angel, the ring belongs to you."

I was breathless, caught up in this world of dreams, of magic, of lost love, of things needing to be made right.

"Fulfill your destiny. Return to the master that loves you and has been waiting for you for so long. The master is near, and he will come take you away from your pitiful life if you but put the..."

I slid the ring onto my finger.

There was a flash of light.

It all happened so fast, yet so slow.

Suddenly, my guide was there.

She pushed my spirit out of my body with a force that knocked me, my spirit me, to the floor.

I looked up, and found my body bathed in a golden glow. *She took possession of my body?* My eyes, large orbs of champagne colored topaz, sparkled brightly in the flickering flames.

"You cannot have her," my guide declared.

Realizing she wasn't talking to me, I followed her piercing feline gaze.

Fear caught in my throat and I choked. A translucent shield of shimmering gold was the only thing standing between us and a humongous floating smoke demon with blazing eyes of fire.

The monster gave a hallow laugh. "You know the rules, guide. She wears my ring. She belongs to me."

About the Author

When Tia Fanning is not lost somewhere in the exciting world of fantasy and romance, you might find her residing in Illinois with her husband, Warren, and two dogs, Drew and Jack.

However, according to her husband, she is usually lost... even the dogs can't find her.

To learn more about Tia and her adventures, visit her at www.tiafanning.com or befriend her on www.myspace.com/tiafanning.

ALSO AVAILABLE FROM RESPLENDENCE PUBLISHING

The Last Celtic Witch by Lyn Armstrong:

"As charming and magical as Celtic legend itself, a truly enjoyable read and wonderful debut!"

Heather Graham
New York Times Bestselling Author

A painful death… a prophecy foretold.

Pursued by evil forces for her powers, recluse Adela MacAye foresees her own agonizing death. She must seek the chosen one to produce an heir and pass on her Celtic powers. To fail would be the end of good magick, plunging the world into darkness.

Conjuring a fertility spell she is led to a sensual chieftain who is betrothed to the sorceress that hunts her. Time is running out as fate and the future pursue her.

Plagued by enemies and undermined by sabotage, handsome Laird Phillip Roberts must save his clan from bloody feud by making an alliance through marriage... a marriage he does not want. After a night of white-hot sensual delights with the alluring witch, his heart commands he break the pledge of peace. With treachery around every corner, will he be too late to save... The Last Celtic Witch?

$4.50 e-book, $12.99 print

The Curse: Book One in the Legend of Blackbeard's Chalice by Maddie James.

"I felt as if I lived every thrilling moment of THE CURSE. Maddie James writes pulse-pounding suspense and riveting romance!"

Teresa Medeiros
New York Times Bestselling Author

Jack Porter is in hot pursuit of his kidnapped wife. Not an easy feat considering it is 1718 and the kidnapper is the notorious pirate, Edward Teach aka. Blackbeard. Determined to rescue his wife, Hannah, and take the pirate's head in the process, Jack sneaks aboard the pirate's ship but is too late. Hannah dies in his arms.

Nearly 300 years later, Claire Winslow vacations on a secluded east coast island, where the image of a man walking the misty shore haunts her. Then he comes to her one night, kisses her, and disappears. The next night they make love and he tells her his name is Jack. But did they really make love? Or was it a dream? And why did he call her Hannah?

The Curse sends Jack and Claire on a wild search through time for a powerful historical artifact – the silver-plated chalice made from Blackbeard's skull. This chalice holds the key to their destiny and their love. Only with the chalice will they be able to reverse Blackbeard's Curse.

Will they find it in time? Or are they destined to be parted by fate once more?

$6.50 e-book, $19.99 print

The Pirate Wench by Melinda Barron

Can a staid, by-the-book journalist find love with a modern day pirate?

Melani Canton is about to find out. When she travels to Florida to be maid-of-honor at her best friend's wedding, she takes on an extra duty: taking a good look at *Ahoy, Matey*, the pirate- themed park where the wedding is set to take place, and writing a story that will attract visitors. While there, she meets handsome swashbuckler, Royce McKenna. Royce is a former lawyer who has given up the courtroom for life on the high seas, amusement park style.

McKenna is the co-owner of *Ahoy, Matey*. When Royce sees Melani he knows that he has to have her. Melani is not, however, the type to sleep with a man she has just met.

So Royce does what any good pirate would do. He "abducts" Melani and gives her a wild night of passion on his pirate ship, where Melani discovers that being Royce's pirate wench isn't such a bad thing. But when the time comes for her to go back to her stoic life, will Royce let her sail off into the sunset? Or will he find a way to keep his Pirate Wench?

$5.50 e-book, $12.99 print

Find Resplendence Titles at the Following Retailers:

Resplendence Publishing:
www.resplendencepublishing.com

Amazon.com: www.amazon.com

Target.com: www.target.com

Fictionwise: www.fictionwise.com

Mobipocket: www.mobipocket.com

All Romance eBooks:
www.allromanceebooks.com

Made in the USA
Charleston, SC
10 November 2010